No Dibs On Murder

ALSO BY LAWRENCE KELTER & FRANK ZAFIRO
The Last Collar
No Dibs on Murder

ALSO BY LAWRENCE KELTER

My Cousin Vinny Series
My Cousin Vinny *Wing and a Prayer*
Back to Brooklyn

Stephanie Chalice Thrillers
(includes the Prequel Series, Main Series, and City Beat Thrillers)
Chloe Mather Thrillers

Other Novels
Counterblow *Season of Faith*
Kiss of the Devil's Breath *Out of Ashes*
Palindrome *Lexa's War*
Encrypting Maya *The Treasure*
Saving Cervantes

As Editor
The Black Car Business Volume 1 *Writers Crushing COVID-19*
The Black Car Business Volume 2

ALSO BY FRANK ZAFIRO
River City series
Stefan Kopriva Mysteries
SpoCompton series
Charlie-316 series (with Colin Conway)
Bricks & Cam Jobs (with Eric Beetner)
The Ania Series (with Jim Wilsky)

Other Novels
The Last Horseman *An Unlikely Phoenix*
Some Degree of Murder (with Colin Conway) *Chisolm's Debt*
The Trade Off (with B.R. Paulson)

LAWRENCE KELTER
&
FRANK ZAFIRO

No Dibs On Murder

Copyright © 2021 by Lawrence Kelter & Frank Scalise

All rights reserved. No part of the book may be reproduced in any form or by any electronic or mechanical means, including information storage and retrieval systems, without permission in writing from the publisher, except by a reviewer who may quote brief passages in a review.

Published by Code 4 Press, an imprint of Frank Zafiro, LLC.

The characters and events in this book are fictitious. Any similarity to real persons, living or dead, is coincidental and not intended by the author

ISBN: 9798733641171:

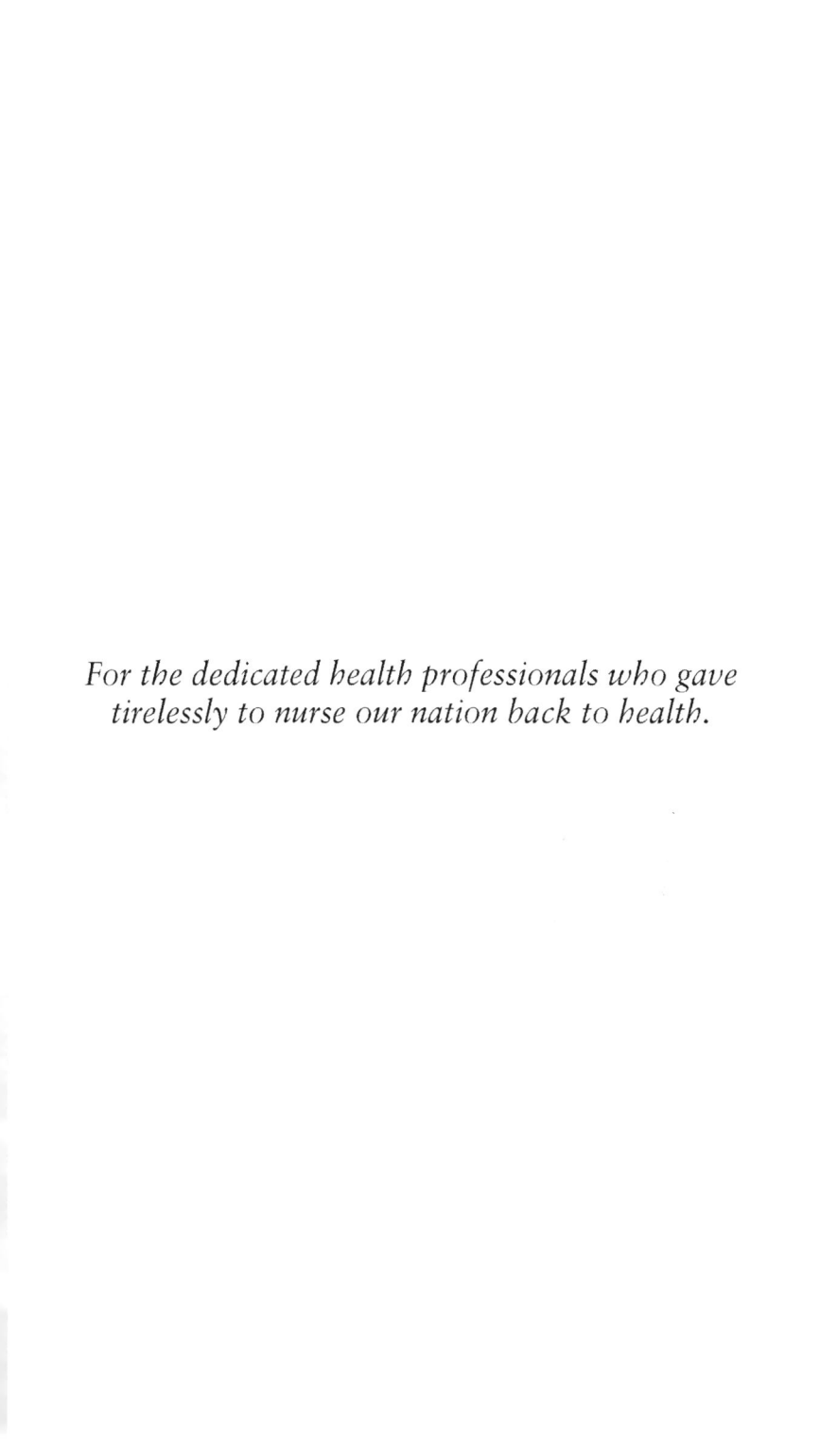

For the dedicated health professionals who gave tirelessly to nurse our nation back to health.

Chapter One

Marty

The small rubber ball slammed into Marty Cohen's forehead, stunning him.

"Jesus!" roared Carson Reynolds from behind him. "Use the racquet, Stitch!"

Marty took a knee, his vision blurring. As his head cleared, the stinging appeared.

"Let's go," Carson urged. "I'm on game point."

"Injury timeout."

"No timeouts, you nancy," Carson boomed. "Come on, man up and finish the game."

Marty shook his head to clear it.

"No?" Carson's voice held a triumphant tone. "Then you forfeit."

"I'm up," Marty said, forcing himself to his feet. Maybe it was the hundred bucks they had on this "friendly" game, or maybe it was because Carson still insisted on calling him Stitch, a nickname he thought he'd left behind in college. Whatever the reason, he moved into position and crouched, signaling his readiness.

"Atta kid," Carson said, suddenly full of camaraderie. "Never say die."

The bigger man bounced the ball precisely three times, then blasted it at the wall.

Marty tried to gauge the trajectory. He shuffled to his right, then realizing he'd misjudged, moved back to his left.

Too late.

The ball clipped him in the nipple this time, making him shriek. His free hand flew to the battered nipple, covering it.

"That's game," Carson pronounced with satisfaction. "And you scream like a ten-year-old girl, Stitch."

Marty rubbed the sore spot. "It hurt, all right? It's a tender place, even for a man. And don't call me Stitch. You know I hate it."

Carson shook his head in either disgust or pity. "You play racquetball like an accountant."

"I *am* an accountant."

"You play racquetball like a *bad* accountant, then."

Marty let his racquet dangle from his wrist on its loop string. "I played you tight."

Carson stood, twirling his racquet repeatedly and catching it. "Tell me something, because I don't understand it."

"You're definitely going to have to narrow that down for me."

"Huh, huh." Carson's deep sarcastic laugh was another holdover from their college days.

Marty glanced around to find the ball. He spotted it in the far corner and went to get it.

"Accounting is math, right?" Carson asked. "I mean, you add and subtract numbers, so it's gotta be math."

"There's math in the process, sure."

2

"And isn't geometry math?"

Marty bent to pick up the ball. "A different kind of math."

"But math."

"Sure."

"So if you do math all day long, and geometry is math, how in the hell can you not eventually figure out how a ball is going to bounce off a wall?"

Marty threw the ball at him.

He missed.

Carson grinned at him as the ball bounced to the opposite corner. "Like I said, you must be a bad accountant."

Marty walked toward the little rubber ball as it rolled to a stop. "You insult people like this down at the dealership?"

"Hell, no. I tell 'em how awesome they are."

"Why can't you do that here?"

"Hey, you want bullshit, come down and buy a car from me. You want truth, come to the gym and play racquetball."

"What I want is a beer."

Carson gave him a thumbs-up. "Now you're talking my language."

Marty scooped up the ball on the way off the court. The next two players stood outside, glaring at them.

"You're two minutes over," said a man in his fifties, his tone a barely disguised snarl.

Marty immediately felt bad. He glanced down at his smart watch to see if the man was right, prepared to apologize.

"And you're about *thirty pounds* over," Carson

said. "So cool your jets."

The man shook his head in disgust. "Asshole."

Carson laughed it off, turning and walking away.

Marty followed. "You shouldn't be such a dick."

"It's two minutes, Marty. And we had a game to finish. Fat Gramps can wait his turn."

It was *his turn*, Marty thought, but instead said, "That guy might come in looking for a new car sometime. You could lose a sale just because you had to be a jerk at the gym."

"Everyone's a jerk at the gym. It's in the contract when you sign up."

Marty snorted.

"Besides," Carson said, "if he comes to the dealership, I'll make a big deal about how he told me what an asshole I was, and make him feel like he got the better of me."

"That works?"

"Sure." Marty heard the bravado in Carson's words, but he could sense something else, too. He wasn't sure exactly what, but it worried him.

They showered quickly and changed clothes. As Marty pulled his wallet from the locker, Carson stuck his hand in his face. "Pay up, Stitch."

"I'll get you at the bar. First round on me."

"You lost. First round is on you already. And a hundred chakalakas."

Marty frowned. He opened up his wallet. A quick count revealed he had a hundred and twelve dollars. He'd have to hope his credit card had enough space on it for the drinks. The way Carson could put 'em away, he wasn't so sure. But Marty still did as he was asked, dropping an even hundred into Carson's open palm.

"That hurts," he admitted.

"Funny. It feels good to me."

"Why do we have to bet, anyway?" Marty complained. "Why can't we just play?"

"Because that would be as boring as your sex life."

"Leave my sex life out of this."

"What sex life?"

Marty sighed. "Maybe we could bet less? Play for pride? Or for beers, like in the commercial."

"Don't be a whiner because you lost."

They walked out into the lobby and started for the door.

Marty was saying, "I know you're, like, king of the gamblers, or whatever, but I just can't afford to—"

That's when he noticed Carson had stopped in his tracks. Marty stopped, too, and turned around, confused. His friend stood frozen, staring past him. Marty followed his gaze. When he saw the object of Carson's fixation, he understood.

The handsome man was cut from the same fit mold as Carson. He wore casual clothing that still managed to look stylish, and walked with a confident, athletic gait. As he passed the check-in desk, he flashed a smile at the two pretty clerks. They tittered and gave him a small wave as he continued toward the door.

Tanner Fritz.

Marty realized he'd clenched his jaw as he stared. He forced himself to relax it, but he couldn't take his eyes off the retreating figure. Beside him, he could feel the hatred coming off of Carson in waves.

Tanner used his fob, and the parking lights of a nearby car blinked. Marty's first reaction was how close the parking space was to the front door, because *of course* Tanner Fritz always managed to get the best spot. He was pretty sure it must have magically opened up right before the man's arrival. Then Marty registered the yellow car that Tanner was getting into.

It was a goddamn Lamborghini.

Son of a *bitch*.

He couldn't believe it. From the exasperated exhale Carson made, he guessed his friend shared the sentiment. Both of them watched as Tanner Fritz started the sports car, backed out of the parking stall, and chirped his tires as the vehicle leapt forward. He was out of sight in about two seconds. Marty was surprised he hadn't left a vapor trail. If he had, it probably would have smelled like Drakkar cologne.

Carson stepped forward to stand at Marty's shoulder. Then he growled, "I fucking *hate* that guy."

Me too, Marty thought. Then he gave voice to the sentiment. "Me, too."

They got beers at the bar and made for a table. Carson led the way. He chose a corner booth, out of the main footpath. This was unusual, Marty noticed. Carson liked to be right in the middle of the action. It maximized his ability to give out his business cards to the men, and to hit on the women.

Maybe he's got a date already, Marty thought.

But when they sat down, Carson surprised him. He was still hung up on the Tanner Fritz sighting. "I fucking hate that guy," he snarled.

"Yeah, you said that."

"Don't you?"

"Of course I do."

Carson shook his head. "I hate the way he prances around, acting like he's God's gift to the world."

"He does act like that," Marty agreed. "Besides, that's *your* job, right?"

"Huh, huh." Carson's sardonic laugh lacked its usual punch. "At least I don't go around ripping people off."

Marty gave him a sideways look.

"What?" Carson asked.

"Nothing." Marty took a sip of his beer.

"No, smartass. What's with the look?"

"What look?"

"The face you made. With that huge red spot on your forehead, it's even more ridiculous, by the way."

Marty touched where the ball had smacked him. "Well, you *do* sell cars for a living."

"So? I don't rip people off."

Marty didn't answer. He sipped his beer and watched Carson over the rim.

"Fine," Carson said. "I don't *blatantly* rip people off. Look, they come to me, they're willing to pay a certain price for a car, and they get that car. They're happy, I'm happy. If they paid a little more than they needed to, so what?"

"Ignorance is bliss, I guess."

"You're damn right." Carson took a long drink

of his beer and shook his head. "But Tanner? He's something else. A whole other level."

"Yeah," Marty agreed, but his mind drifted to something other than the version of Tanner Fritz who strutted out of the gym. Instead, he recalled happier times—the five of them in college, young and full of promise. How they refused to go home for Thanksgiving senior year, and spent the holiday weekend together on campus. Rather than succumb to the duty of being with the family they were born into, each of them decided to be with the family they chose. It was the first true act of adulthood Marty could point to in his own life, and one of the best weekends ever.

Of course, that was before he met Andrea. And then Tanner snatched her away from him.

Carson's eyes narrowed. "That's all you've got, Stitch? *Yeah?* This guy cons me out of millions of dollars and steals your wife, and all you've got is *yeah?*"

"Fuck him," Marty said, trying to redeem himself.

"That's a little better, I guess." Carson took another slug of his beer. "How does a guy like that live with himself? I mean, does he get up every day, look in the mirror, and think, 'Hey, I'm a great guy?' or some shit like that?"

Marty thought about it even though he didn't want to. Andrea's departure was less than two years old, and it still stung. He shrugged. "I think he's always looked in the mirror and liked what he saw."

"Probably. I just don't remember him being all *God's gift to the world* in college." Carson said.

"That's because you're the same way."

Carson's eyes narrowed.

"*Were* the same way," Marty corrected himself.

Carson's scowl subsided slightly. "Things were different back then."

"Sure. We were kids."

"We were more like brothers, all of us."

"And sister," Marty said. "Don't forget Serena."

Carson gave him a sly look. "How could I?" He tapped his forehead. "I've got every inch of her catalogued right here."

Marty rolled his eyes. "And what was her major in college?"

"Sociology."

"Nope."

"Political Science, then."

"Wrong again."

"Then I don't remember."

"My point, exactly. And it was psychology, by the way."

Carson shrugged. "That was school. It was years ago."

"How about her favorite movie, then? Or her favorite song?"

"Who cares?"

"Not you, obviously."

Carson gave him a suspicious look. "Have you got the hots for her or something?"

"No. I just know a thing or two about my friends."

"Well, yippy-skippy for you. Maybe if you'd known a thing or two about your wife, she wouldn't have bounced."

Marty looked down, clenching his jaw again. *It*

wasn't my fault, he thought. How was he supposed to compete with Tanner-goddamn-Fritz? The man was tall, rich, full of muscles, and photogenic enough for a billboard underwear ad. Marty was short, barely scraping by, skinny, and every picture taken of him made it look like he was about to have a stroke.

Still, Carson didn't have to rub it in.

His friend seemed to sense that he'd stepped over the line. "Sorry," he mumbled. "I didn't mean what I said. I just get so pissed off whenever I think about that asshole."

"I know."

"I was *that* close," Carson said, holding up his thumb and forefinger to signify exactly how close he meant. "But that snake bought me out for pennies on the dollar, and then turned around and sold out for millions."

It was actually tens of millions, but Marty didn't think Carson would appreciate the correction.

"I helped build that company from the start up," Carson went on. "Yeah, that asshole had a few ideas, but so did I. Not only that, I reeled in all of the clients. The fuel that a company runs on is cash flow, and that comes from clients. I made sure we had plenty of fuel. Santo Corp never would have bought the company if it wasn't for what I did."

"True," Marty said. "But if you think about it, there never would have been a company at all if it weren't for those brainstorming sessions all five of us had in college. We all contributed."

"Sure, but that was just talk. Tanner and me went out and actually made it happen. Besides, it wasn't like the rest of you got screwed over. You got contract work from us once we were up and running. Barry got the IT position. And we hired Serena to run HR. None of you lost your stake, not like I did."

Marty gaped at him. "I lost my wife."

"Plenty of fish in the sea, brother."

"Plenty of dollars in the pot," Marty shot back.

"No." Carson shook his head again. "Those were *my* dollars."

"And that was *my* wife."

Carson reconsidered. "Okay, I see your point. Either way, that son of a bitch won. He cheated and stole from us, and now he's driving around in a goddamn yellow Lamborghini."

Marty's jaw tightened. The Lamborghini *did* make it worse somehow.

"We should fucking kill him," Carson said.

"Amen," Marty said, raising his glass.

Carson didn't move. He only stared at Marty, anger plastered on his face. Then he repeated, more slowly, "We. Should. Fucking. *Kill* him."

"Yeah, right."

Carson stared at him, tight lipped.

Marty lowered his glass. "Wait, are you serious?"

Carson deliberately lifted his own glass and clinked it lightly against Marty's. "Serious as a heart attack."

Chapter Two

Carson

"I wish I still smoked," Serena mumbled dreamily.

Carson stared up at the bedroom ceiling, still catching his breath.

"You've still got the motion down," he said. "That's for sure."

She pinched the skin nearest her hand, which lay on his chest. She caught nipple, twisting a little harder than he liked.

"Hey!"

Serena didn't apologize. She returned her hand to the center of his chest.

Carson rubbed the sore spot. "You've got me sounding like Stitch, all whiny and nipple hurt."

"Did you pinch him there, too?"

"Huh Huh. No, I blasted the ball into the wall and he spazzed into it."

"Sure you weren't aiming to hit him there?"

"I was trying to win the game."

"Mmmmm," was all she said, and he could never tell if that sound meant skepticism or disapproval. It bothered him that it mattered at all, but somehow it did. His mother should be the only woman he really cared about when it came to approval.

"Not that Stitch was any competition," he said.

"He doesn't like it when you call him that."

"Sure, he does."

"No, he doesn't. He hates it."

Carson frowned. "It's his nickname."

"It was," she agreed. "But he hates it."

"How do you know?"

"How do you *not* know?"

Carson thought about that. He couldn't remember Marty ever objecting to his nickname before. "I think you're wrong."

"I'm not. It's just that you're kind of an asshole."

She said it easily, and without judgment, but it irked him just the same. "*I'm* a good guy."

"Everyone thinks that about themselves." Serena patted his chest and sat up. She swung her legs over the edge of the bed and reached for her panties. "It's called a lack of self-awareness."

"I'm very self-aware."

"Mmmmmm."

Serena slid her legs into her panties and stood.

That's a perfect ass, he thought. *A goddamn gold medal winner.* He enjoyed it for a moment. It had been several months since they'd taken advantage of the benefits part of their friendship, and he now realized how much he'd needed it. It felt like a win, and other than crushing Marty at racquetball, he hadn't been getting many of those lately.

Then he came back to their conversation, and insisted, "I'm the most self-aware guy I know."

"I believe you."

She retrieved her bra and shrugged herself into it, expertly snapping the hook into place. He admired her perfectly cradled breasts. Then another image intruded, and he scowled.

"You want to talk about who's an asshole?" he asked. "I'll tell you who. Tanner-goddamn-Fritz is an asshole."

Serena glanced over her shoulder at him. "Why are you bringing him up?"

"We saw him leaving the gym today."

"Yeah?" She turned back to finding the rest of her clothes, stepping into her skirt and zipping it. "What'd he say?"

"Nothing. We didn't talk to the son of a bitch. We just saw him prancing out of the gym to his car." Carson frowned. "You know what he's driving now?"

"The silver Lexus?"

"He has a Lexus now?"

Serena nodded, looking for her blouse. She found it on the floor near the foot of the bed, halfway under. "An LS-something. He got it a few months ago."

"LS-500?"

"That's it."

"Are you fucking kidding me?" Carson muttered. *The guy must be swimming in cash*, he thought.

"So, not the Lexus, then?" Serena pulled on the blouse, adjusting the fit.

"No." Carson couldn't believe he was actually having this conversation. "It was a Lamborghini."

"Is that more expensive than a Lexus?"

"Two or three times more, depending on the model." He shook his head in disgust. "But when you rip people off, I guess you can afford all the expensive cars you want."

"Now, *that* sounds like whining."

"I'm not whining," Carson whined. As soon as he heard his own voice, he stopped and ground his teeth. "That guy's just a complete asshole. Assholes shouldn't win."

"Assholes win all the time." Serena retrieved her shoes, and sat back down on the edge of the bed. "Maybe they win *because* they're assholes."

"Jesus, you're a frosty bitch sometimes. I'm pouring my heart out to you here."

She cast a sardonic glance over her shoulder. "I'm a frosty bitch because I don't want to listen to you complain?"

"We just finished making love," Carson said. "Isn't that supposed to make you feel all tender or something?"

"We just finished fucking," she specified, putting on her shoes. "And you're not big enough to make me feel tender."

"Fuck you!" Carson flared. Serena always seemed to know how to get under his skin.

"No thanks," she said evenly. "I'm good."

Carson stewed for a moment while she slipped on her shoes. He knew she was going to leave shortly, so he tried to keep the conversation going a little longer. "What's the difference, anyway?"

"Between making love and fucking?"

"Yeah."

"I'm not sure either of us is qualified to answer that. But for what it's worth, I don't feel tender-hearted. I feel marginally satisfied, and late for getting out of here before you turn into a blubbering man-child."

"Huh huh," he guffawed without much conviction. "I'm serious."

"So am I."

"This is how you treat your...?" he trailed off, not sure what he was to her exactly.

"Occasional fuck buddy?" she offered.

He frowned. They were more than that, weren't they? "Well... I mean, we're friends, too."

Serena stood and smoothed her skirt. "Okay, Carson, then as a friend, I'm here to tell you that unless you're Woody Allen, women don't think whining is sexy. So knock it off."

"Seriously? You think Woody Allen is sexy?"

"No, but my mom did."

"That wimpy clown—I wouldn't think he could get laid in a brothel."

Serena ticked off a few names on her fingertips, "Mia Farrow, Penelope Cruz, Scarlett Johansson ... need I go on?"

"So he had a few sexy costars. So what?"

She frowned. "Read a scandal sheet, would ya?"

Carson sat up, propping a pillow behind him. The sheet fell away as he did so, but he left it. He was always of a mind to let your best assets show. "Point taken. And I wasn't whining. I was bitching."

"What's the difference? Aside from the misogyny?"

"The what?"

Serena sighed. "I have to go."

"Stay a while," he said, trying to keep the pleading out of his voice. "I'll be ready for another round soon. We can order in some Chinese after."

"Too late. I'm dressed now."

"Fine." He tried to sound like he didn't care, but was pretty sure he hadn't carried it off.

Serena gave him a flat, forced smile and started to leave. Then she turned back to him. "Look, Carson, you've got to let this go. Get on with your life. You can't let this keep eating at you."

Carson let her words rattle around in his brain for a few moments. He waited to see if they gained any traction. Maybe she was right. There was a time when he and Tanner were as close as two bros could be. That was why the betrayal hurt so much, and hit so hard. It started the downward trajectory of the last two years of his life. He'd gone from a big shot at an up-and-coming company one minute, to working at a car dealership the next. He wasn't even the sales manager at the dealership anymore. He had to work the floor as a salesman, scrambling for commissions.

Let it go?

Not a chance.

"Easy for you to say," he said. "You still have your cushy job, just like before. You have your salary and enough vacation time to go off on antiquing trips and whatever other bullshit, and life is still the same for you. It's a lot different for me."

"Life changes all the time, for everyone."

"And my life change was I got screwed over by my supposed best friend."

"I mean it. Let it go. It's the only way you'll get back to being yourself again." She shrugged. "If that's who you want to be."

"Of course that's what I want." He frowned. "Who the hell else would I want to be?"

She didn't answer.

Carson rubbed his chin, rolling her words over in his mind. She waited for a few seconds, but he knew she wouldn't give him much time. He'd called her a frosty bitch because he was frustrated, but the truth was, while she was playful about sex, Serena *was* cold. It was one of the things he dug about her.

"I don't know if I *can* get over it," he finally admitted.

"You have to."

"What if I can't?"

"Then you wither and die as a human being." She turned away and headed toward the door.

"Or I could just kill him," Carson called after her.

Serena stopped. She turned around slowly, then walked back to the foot of the bed. Her eyes were alive with curiosity and something more that he couldn't entirely place. "Have you ever killed anyone before?" she asked.

"Of course not."

Disappointment overcame her expression. "Then you're just talking shit."

He shook his head. "No, I'm serious. Stitch and I talked about it at the bar."

She dropped her chin and stared at him. "You planned a murder at a public bar? After playing racquetball?"

"After seeing Tanner-goddamn-Fritz leave in a yellow-fucking-Lamborghini—yeah, we did."

"And you're serious?"

"As a heart attack," Carson said figuring that the line seemed to work on Marty, so it was worth a try here, too.

Serena continued to stare at him, not smiling.

"What?" he finally asked.

"You're *not* serious," she said.

"I am. We are."

"Why?"

"How can you ask me that? He stole the business we built together. He bought me out for pennies on the dollar, then turned around and sold it to a megacorporation for millions of dollars."

"Mmmmm."

"Oh, that's not enough?" Carson waved his hands. "He stole Stitch's wife!"

"You can't *steal* a woman. This isn't *Game of Thrones*. He didn't hit her over the head with a club and drag her off by her hair. She made a choice."

"You know what I mean. And he did hit her over the head... with his bank account. No matter how you slice it, she was married and he seduced her."

"She made a choice."

"Try and tell Marty that Tanner didn't steal her. See how far you get."

"So Marty wants to kill him over that?"

"Yeah, he does." He didn't mention that Marty was still wavering even after several beers. Carson knew he could eventually convince him. "We both do." He peered at her closely, trying to pierce her flat expression. "You don't think we're serious?"

"I think you're stupid, that's what I think."

"Why?"

"Any idea hatched in a bar is *prima facie* stupid," Serena said.

Carson didn't answer. He didn't like it when she used words he didn't know, and besides that, it was his opinion that the best ideas he'd ever had originated over drinks at a bar.

"For another thing, your murder plan is three hours old and you're already blabbing about it."

"I'm telling *you*. I'm not blabbing."

"Who else have you told?"

"No one. And I'm not going to, either. You know why?"

She shook her head slightly. "Tell me."

"Because we *are* serious. That son of a bitch deserves to be killed, and we're going to do it."

Serena smiled slightly. Usually the most he saw from her was a smirk, so an actual smile surprised him. Even so, her eyes didn't join in. Instead, they held a flat, almost reptilian quality. That was the coldness in her at play, he realized. Then the reason she was probably smiling occurred to him, and he looked away, irritation flashing.

"Get out of here," he said, waving his hand at her. "You and your stupid smile."

Serena didn't move. "You really are serious, aren't you?"

"I told you."

"I know, and that was stupid. You tell people, you'll get caught."

"What do you care?"

"Because I don't want to go to prison."

His gaze snapped back to her. "What?"

Her lips parted and her teeth showed, shark-like. Then she said, "I want in."

Carson stared, shocked. His mouth fell open. "Uhhhhhhh... you...?"

"I want in," she repeated. "And that means you

two mopes are going to have start listening to me so that we don't get arrested."

Carson shook his head sharply to clear it. Then he asked, "Why? What's your beef with him?"

"With Tanner-goddamn-Fritz?"

"Yeah."

"All that matters," Serena said, "is that I'm in, and I'll make sure you two don't screw it up."

Carson thought about it. Should he let her into their scheme? Besides himself, he felt Serena was one of the smartest people he knew. And if she was in, that'd convince Marty not to back out. Besides, she already knew about it, so having her as part of the group was safer.

He held out his hand. "Okay."

Serena glanced down at his proffered hand, then put a knee onto the bed, and leaned forward to give it a quick shake. As usual, Carson took advantage of the situation to glance down her blouse. Also as usual, he was impressed by her firm grip. It was pretty good for a human resources manager.

When she stood back up, she said, "Let's get together tomorrow night to work out the details."

"All right. Where?"

"Here at your place. You can order the Chinese you promised me."

"That was for getting laid."

"Yeah, well this is better."

"How?" In his experience, nothing rated higher than sex.

"It's revenge," she said. "And revenge is better than sex." She turned and walked out of his bedroom.

"Serena!" he called through the open door.
"What?"
"Why do you hate him?"

She glanced over her shoulder at him with those flat eyes. "Why do you care? Fuck off." She disappeared around the corner. A moment later, he heard the front door open and shut behind her.

"Fuck off," Carson muttered. Then he shrugged.

It was as good a reason as any.

Chapter Three

Barry

Barry Young looked out at the two hundred programmers and IT professionals that Chismo now employed. They sat side by side in rows of ten, five rows deep—fifty to a floor in a commercial building that its parent company owned. Despite Santo Corp absorbing Chismo into the fold two years ago, Barry still thought of himself strictly as a Chismo man. He liked who he was then better than who he was now.

Unlike the others, Barry did not have a desk of his own. He didn't want one and since the accident, he couldn't sit still in one had it been assigned to him. This inability to sit at a desk had given rise to the nickname "Roamer," as he spent all day drifting from one workstation to the next, helping, advising, and problem-solving before moving on.

"In-in-intuh-tuh-ger overfl-fl-flow," he said in his soft-spoken voice as his head bobbed up and down, a continuous confirmation that he was sure of the fix he proposed.

"Integer overflow?" Clyde, one of the programmers asked.

"Y-y-yes," Barry confirmed.

"You're sure?"

Barry grunted his reply to avoid having to speak.

The words sprang from his mind in rapid-fire, only to stumble when they reached his lips. The way his stutter made him sound unsure of himself both embarrassed and enraged him at the same time.

Clyde studied the screen in front of him. "Where?"

Barry leaned forward and pointed to a line of code, his head bobbing more dramatically. "H-here. Vuh-vuh-vuh…" He paused, concentrating. "Vuh-value too large."

Don't make me explain more, Clyde. You've got a goddamn degree in software engineering, so use it.

Clyde reread the code, then did some quick math on a notepad. "I'll be damned. Thanks, Roamer. Sometimes I don't know what I'd do without you."

A stab of anger in Barry dulled the compliment. "Wuh-wuh-waste more t-t-time, probably," he said, before moving on. He could feel Clyde's befuddled stare on him as he drifted to find the next problem. He ignored Clyde. His own level of frustration these past two years was constant. People like Clyde missing obvious solutions was one reason. Barry had been a talented programmer out of college, but had become even more mathematically adept after the accident, a condition his doctors called savant syndrome. As a result, he lacked patience for the inability of others to resolve what seemed to him to be simple challenges.

At the same time, the other effects of the accident were a constant source of irritation. His interpersonal skills were all but lost and he struggled with basic nonanalytical concepts he never thought twice about in the past. Common expressions seemed to bend his mind in a direction it didn't want to go. This difficulty was exacerbated by the frustration that even when his mind formed those perfect thoughts, they became tangled in his mouth when tried to express them.

He wandered toward the windows at the end of the row and stood for several minutes, straining to gain control of his roiling emotions. The light struck the glass in a way that showed his ethereal reflection. The stolid countenance staring back at him belied all of the painful sentiments churning below the surface. He barely registered the hum of conversation and the clattering of keyboards behind him. Only when the sound of voices suddenly fell did he break away from his reverie.

Barry turned to see Tanner Fritz walk off the elevator.

"How are you doing?" Tanner asked over and over as he made the rounds on his daily walkthrough. It was his standard operating procedure, Barry knew. The big shot boss reserved twenty minutes every day to show his face to the peasants and pretend that he was interested in their work.

Barry wiped at his mouth and watched, his anger surging back up. This time, though, it was tempered with a bitter sorrow. There was a time he would have called Tanner his best friend. A time when he believed that anything was possible.

"How are you doing? What's new?" Up and down the aisles Tanner went. "How are you doing, George? What's new, Gwen?"

Of course, Barry thought. Of course, he knew

everyone's name and the single most important thing in each of their lives. What else did he have to do while sitting in his big office upstairs besides memorize such things?

"Complete the ten K this weekend, Bruce? Your little guy over his cold, Juan?"

Barry saw it all as an act but others were charmed by him. He saw the result. Everyone felt more important after his daily visit. The uptick in productivity proved this.

Tanner reached Barry. "Solving the mysteries of the universe, Bare?" Tanner put an arm over his shoulder and tapped lightly on his temple. "What's going on in there, my friend?"

If you only knew, Barry thought. But there was no way he could express all the anger, sadness, and regret flying around in his skull. And even if he found the words, they'd only stumble out of his mouth, taking forever.

"You're a superstar, Barry," Tanner said. "A damn superstar."

"T-t-hanks," Barry managed flatly.

"I mean it. People appreciate the help." Tanner leaned a little closer. "Just remember to be nice, too, huh? People appreciate that, too."

Nice? Barry stared at him in disbelief. After everything that had happened, Tanner had the audacity to ask him to be *nice*?

"Y-y-you…" he sputtered. His mouth refused to conform, and he clenched his jaw in frustration.

As was routine, Serena Trowers followed Tanner from floor to floor each day when he made the rounds of the four bullpens. Tanner waved her over.

"Serena," Tanner said smoothly, "would you be kind enough to take Barry to the break room for a cup of tea? He seems a little … off."

Barry shook Tanner's arm off his shoulder. "L-l-looking for a s-soft sp-sp-spot?" he asked.

"Pardon?" Tanner asked, seemingly unsure of what he'd heard.

To plunge the knife, Barry wanted to say, but the words remained locked behind his lips. He walked away to intercept Serena. "B-b-brutus says I need a cup of tea," he told her. The words always came easier around Serena. "G-g-get me the hell out of here!"

Chapter Four

Serena

Serena led Barry into the elevator, waiting until the doors slid closed before grinning at him. The two of them always shared a unique connection. She may have shared a particular loyalty to Marty the lost puppy and occasionally shared her bed with Carson but she always shared her *soul* with Barry. Or at least as much of it as she was willing to reveal. Barry was the one who understood that part of her, and so he knew her as well as anyone could. Serena often wondered if anyone could truly understand her, her secret thoughts and the demons that drove her. Some of her best friends, straightforward girls married for years, complained to her that their husbands didn't know what made them tick. Serena was not straightforward, not simple by any stretch of the imagination, and none of the men in her life truly knew what made her tick. None of them knew about her secret hobbies or her adventurous trips away from home. Her secret life was hers alone and not a one of them suspected.

Barry, though, she thought. *If anyone is capable of truly seeing me, it's him.*

At the break room, she prepared tea for them both. "You should smile at Tanner once in a while," she said while filling his cup. "He can't read your mind. He doesn't know what you're thinking."

"L-l-lucky f-for him," Barry said.

Serena handed him the cup and set about making her own. "You don't have to mean it. A smile can say *I like you* to his face and *I want to set you on fire* to you." These days, Barry's expression could carry this off easily.

From his ticks and affectations there was no way of telling how he had interpreted the comment. He held the cup of tea she had prepared for him without sipping. "F-f-fire," Barry repeated. "S-s-set him-m-m on f-fire."

"You'd like that, wouldn't you—see him go up in a ball of flames?"

Barry bobbed his head. His lips twisted painfully, but no words came. She knew how hard it was for him, even with her. Then she noticed his ticks getting worse the longer he sat. Looking around the empty break room, she placed her hand on his. "Get up and walk around if you need to. It's just you and me."

He rose like an elevator car jerked skyward by a thick steel cable. "S-sure. I'll walk."

She placed his teacup on the table and watched as he began making a perfect rectangle around the room turning at each corner only when he ran out of floor. She studied his expression. Once, she'd been capable of reading him clearly. Now it was anyone's guess. His eyes were no longer a window to his soul. "Penny for your thoughts," she said.

"My ass," he whooped.

"Huh?"

"My ass," he repeated.

"My ass or your ass?" she asked with a grin.

"Su-super star, my ass." He pointed. "Tanner's fault."

"Your ass is Tanner's fault?"

"Not f-f-funny." He glanced away but not before she saw what looked like anger and hurt in his eyes.

She sidled up to him and rubbed the length of his arm. "What's the matter, hon?"

He shook his head, not looking at her.

"Tell me," she urged him.

Barry kept his gaze averted. His jaw worked, and slowly the words spilled out. "I u-u-sed to be the m-m-man," he said, struggling through the sentence. "Th-th-then T-t-tanner ch-ch-cheaped out and..." He trailed off.

She wasn't sure if it was emotion or just his natural difficulty with speaking that forced the pause. "He cheaped out on the server move, and you paid the price."

Wordlessly, Barry nodded.

"What can I do to help?" she asked.

"P-p-push Tanner."

She grimaced. "What? You want me to push him?"

Barry nodded. "D-d-down a flight of st-st-stairs."

"Really? That would make you happy?"

He nodded again, his expression resolute.

Serena remained quiet for a while, thinking. She checked her watch. "Close enough to take lunch," she pronounced. "Grab your jacket, hon. We need to talk."

She led him outside. Barry followed without question.

The Chismo building was situated in an industrial park, one of eight buildings arranged in a circle facing a man-made pond with benches placed around the perimeter. It was only 11:40 when they reached the campus area but the food trucks were already arriving: Mexican, deli, pizza, dogs, and a dessert truck.

"What are you having?" Serena asked as she took in the line of food trucks assembled in the parking lot.

"T-two big d-dogs."

"*Two?*" she asked with a smile.

"And a beer."

"A beer for lunch? You're really stepping out, aren't you?" She raised her eyebrows.

Barry stared back at her, inscrutable.

"You've got a full afternoon ahead of you. Are you sure?"

"I c-can handle it. What about y-you?"

"I was thinking about a dog with the works too. But no beer."

"B-b-bullsh-shit. Get us a s-s-seat. I'll g-get you a beer." He started off toward the food truck.

Serena made her way to a bench in the shade, passing between two buildings. On the way, a flash of bright yellow caught her eye. Dazzling sunlight reflected of the Lamborghini's windshield causing her to shield her eyes. It was parked in Tanner's spot, coned off from all the other cars in the executive's section of the lot. *Huh. So that's the phallic symbol the boys are so worked up about. Can't say I blame them.*

Off in the distance she heard Barry barking at the

food vendor, "Dogs, b-big dogs—foot longs."

A raspy exhaust burble caught her by surprise. Tanner was behind the wheel of the bright yellow sports car revving it so loudly that a tree-full of crows took off skyward. It looked like a scene from an Alfred Hitchcock movie. "A-hole," she muttered just as Barry returned and shoved a foot long hot dog in her face.

"Careful," she said. "You get mustard on my blouse and I'll murder you."

"Bull-bull ... BS. I know you. You l-l-love me."

"I don't love anyone," she said, but raised the food. "Thanks for the dog, though."

He handed her a bottle of beer in a brown paper bag.

"Brilliant disguise," she mocked gently. "Who would be smart enough to figure out I've got twelve ounces of lager in here?"

Barry's cheeks were distended as he chewed a hefty chunk of his dog. "F-f-fuck 'em," he said. "If… c-can't take a j-joke."

The exhaust burble slowed when the Lamborghini came out of idle and into reverse. Serena pointed out the car with Tanner in the driver's seat. Once out of the spot the car bolted forward as it screamed through the parking lot. "The prick got rich on the sale to Santo. A Lexus, now a Lamborghini, too… what's next? Don't you just hate him?"

Barry grunted and continued to wolf down the hot dog.

Have to take it slower, she told herself.

Barry had certain talents to bring to table, though

neither Carson nor Marty might see it that way. She could convince them, but she had to convince Barry first.

Serena's gaze drifted as she watched the men and women walking around the pond looking for spots to enjoy their lunch. "You ever people watch? Wonder what they're thinking?" she asked.

"P-p-people suck."

"Sure, but watching them is fun. I love it." She picked out a woman on a blanket propped up against the stump of an elm tree. "See her, the way her legs are locked one over the other and the look of worry on her face? She just took a pregnancy test in the employee bathroom."

"P-positive?" he asked.

"Mos def."

"Sh-sh-should be h-ha-appy."

"Not if she cheated on her husband and isn't sure who knocked her up."

"You know?"

"Just guessing. That's the point. It's a game, Barry." She motioned toward a slender man walking in their direction on his way back to one of the buildings. The top of his head was completely bald but the hair on his temples was as thick as broadloom carpeting. "See him?"

"Sure. Sure."

"Definite serial killer. He's got twelve bodies buried in the crawlspace under his home." The two of them followed the man as he strode confidently toward the entrance. Then she mused, "I wonder if we asked nicely if he'd make Tanner number thirteen."

Barry stopped chewing. "S-serious? You hate him enough to..."

She picked up the paper bag and took a quick swig of beer before nestling it where it couldn't easily be seen. "Yeah. I do and I'm not the only one. Marty and Carson feel the same way."

Barry blinked, but didn't answer.

She pressed forward gently. "Carson feels like Tanner cheated him out of a fortune. And as far as Marty's concerned, Tanner stole his wife."

Barry remained silent, his expression vacant.

"What about you, hon?"

He blinked again but remained silent.

"Oh, come on. You of all people, Barry, should understand. I figure you want him dead more than anyone else. You pleaded with him to have pros build the server room and what did you get for insisting? He cheaped out and an eight hundred pound server bank fell on your head and almost crushed you to death. I can't believe you don't want him dead."

"I *do* want him dead," Barry said suddenly. "He took *me*."

Serena smiled grimly. "There it is, then. So you want in on this?"

"Th-th-this?"

"Don't play dumb," she chided, reaching out and tapping him on the forehead. "I know everything in there works, probably better than before. What's your hang up?"

"I d-d-*don't* want to go to j-j-jail."

"You, Barry, you're a pussy."

"Don't want B-b-bubba using my a-a-sass f-f-for

one."

"What if I could promise you we'd never get caught?"

"H-h-how-how can you p-p-promise?"

"I'm working on it, hon. Can we count you in?"

Barry's neck stiffened. He brushed crumbs off his lap onto the ground, then gazed off into the distance, avoiding eye contact.

Did I push him too far?

It didn't matter. She was all-in now, and the three of them would have to be as well. She'd make sure of it.

Chapter Five

Marty

The foursome sat in Carson's living room, avoiding each others' gaze. Out of the corner of his eye, Marty noticed Carson bouncing his knee nervously. Barry stared at the wall, perfectly still. Only Serena seemed somewhat at ease, but even she had an air of impatience about her.

"Suddenly no one wants to say anything?" She looked pointedly at Carson, then at Marty. "Were you guys just talking tough before? Is that it?"

"No," Carson said, his tone mopey but resolute. "I was serious."

"Me, too," Marty said cautiously. "I mean, I thought I was. It's just that... well..."

"Well, what?"

"Being pissed off and talking is one thing. It blows off steam. This... is more serious."

"Really, Marty? You're wussing out?" Serena shook her head in disgust.

Beside her, Carson gave him a disdainful look. "Don't be a pussy. This was your idea."

"*My* idea? You were the one who said—"

"It doesn't matter whose idea it was," Serena interrupted. "We're here now. So let's talk about it."

No one answered. Carson went back to bouncing

his knee. Barry stared. Serena gave each of them dirty looks in turn. The tension in the room mounted until he couldn't take it any longer.

"Fine!" Marty said. "I'll say it."

"Say what?" Serena asked.

"What we're all thinking."

"We're all thinking you're a dildo," Carson said.

"Heh. Marty's a dildo," chuckled Barry.

"I'm not a dildo."

"Yeah, you are. But one of those half-hard ones that don't satisfy. Right, Serena?"

Serena glared at him. "You know a lot about not satisfying a woman?"

Carson looked momentarily stricken. "No."

"I'm not a dildo!" Marty repeated. "That's not what everyone was thinking."

"I was," Carson said.

"M-m-me, too," Barry added.

Serena looked at him, and shrugged.

Marty sighed. He looked around with a sharp gaze, then said in a hushed tone, "Wiii-errrr."

Carson's eyes narrowed. "Why her?" He glanced at Serena. "She's our friend, that's why."

"No," Marty said. "I said—"

"Then again," Carson continued, "you might have a point. Why *do* you want Tanner dead, Serena?"

"Why do you care? Fuck off."

Carson wagged a finger. "Now I see your point, Marty."

"Wire!" Marty yelled. "I said *wire*."

"Wire," Barry repeated.

"Wire what?" Carson asked him.

Marty turned up his hands in an 'are you kidding me here' gesture.

"Marty's worried one of us is wearing a wire," Serena said calmly. "You fucking idiot."

"Thank you," Marty said.

"I was talking to you."

Marty looked hurt.

Carson frowned. "Why would anyone—*ohhhhh*." He looked around at the three of them suspiciously, his gaze settling on Marty. "You actually think someone went to the cops? Why would someone do that?"

"I don't know," Marty said. "But before we talk about doing you know what to you know goddamn who, maybe we should be sure."

"G-g-good idea," Barry said. "Safety protocol."

"So, what?" Carson asked. "Do we all, like, frisk each other or something? Because if so, I call—"

"Serena," Marty said quickly.

"—Serena," Carson finished. He scowled. "I already called it, Stitch."

"I said her name first."

"What are you, nine?"

"No, I'm a fully grown man."

"Well," Carson said. "Half-grown. A half-grown man who just called dibs."

"Who *beat* you at dibs," Marty corrected.

"No, I started first. You can't interject like that."

"Show me in the rules where it says that."

"Everyone knows it says that."

"No, they don't."

"Yeah, they do." He glanced at Barry. "Tell him, Barry."

"N-n-no handb-b-book for dibs," Barry said. "B-b-both of you are disqualified. I c-c-call Serena."

Carson leveled his finger at Barry. "Shut up, Barry. No one asked you."

Serena stood without a word. Unceremoniously, she kicked off her shoes and peeled her shirt over her head, revealing her bra.

Marty stared at her flat stomach. He let his eyes drift upward, pausing at her breasts cradled in black lace.

"I just *knew* it was black," Marty whispered, feeling a stir in his loins.

Then he glanced up at her face. She gave him a reproving stare, and he looked away.

Damn, she can kill with those looks, Marty thought.

A moment later, Serena wriggled out of her jeans, and Marty looked back. The denim pooled around her ankles, and she stepped from them lithely. Then she did a slow turn.

"Black panties, too," Marty said quietly. "I fucking knew it."

His excitement was full on now. Serena had always been his fantasy girl, even more so because she'd been real, right there, just tantalizingly close. Of course, he'd seen her in a swimsuit dozens of times, but this was somehow different. It was more illicit.

Then Carson ruined it.

"I could've told you they were black," he said, his voice smug and knowing.

A tickle of jealousy rippled in Marty's chest, but he didn't let it take hold. Instead, he admired the curve of Serena's hip as she turned. In his considered opinion, she was even more beautiful than she was in college.

Serena stopped turning. "You see any wires?"

"No," Carson said.

"N-n-no," Barry said.

"No," Marty said. "But transmitters today can be pretty small, so maybe you should—"

Serena shot him a dangerous look and he shut up.

She snapped her fingers. "Let's go, boys. This isn't supposed to be a peep show. Get stripped or get out your dollar bills."

All three men sat still, thinking it over.

"The dollar bills part was a joke," she said acidly. "Lose the clothes, gentlemen. I want to see bulges. Let's get this wire nonsense over with."

Marty stood slowly. He hunched slightly to disguise his ardor. Beside him, Carson stripped off unabashedly, never afraid to strut his muscles or his package. Barry moved more deliberately. Marty figured that had to do with the injury. He hadn't seen Barry move fast since before the accident. Even so, Marty quickly fell behind, waiting for his flag to refurl.

"Let's go, Stitch," Carson said impatiently. "I want to get on with this."

Marty stepped out of his jeans and made a show of folding them. He was halfway through when Carson knocked them out of his hands. The jeans flopped onto the coffee table, the belt buckle clunking against the surface.

He was still at half-mast and furiously trying to think of dead puppies and baseball statistics. Serena noticed his problem and gave him a look that could have been disgust or amusement.

"Anyone see anything?" she asked.

All three men gave each other a cursory glance.

"Nope," Carson said.

"Uh-uh," grunted Marty.

"No w-w-w-ires," Barry said, "but M-m-marty's got a chubby."

And that was all it took. Marty fizzled like a deflated balloon. He couldn't remember ever being so happy at losing an erection before.

"No, I don't."

Serena made a point of looking again. "For your sake, I sure hope that's not fully loaded."

"It's not."

"It was before," Carson said. "Barry saw."

Barry nodded sagely.

Marty flashed Barry a dirty look. "You were supposed to be looking for wires, dick."

"You've got a weird kink there, Stitch." Carson shook his head. "But whatever floats your raft, man."

"I don't have a kink," Marty protested.

"Maybe you need one."

"And maybe you need another three inches to get off the junior varsity team," Serena said pointedly.

Carson's smile faded. "I hate basketball."

"Who said anything about basketball?"

Serena reached for her jeans. All three men followed suit. Marty didn't meet anyone's gaze as he zipped up and pulled his shirt over his head. He didn't bother tucking it in. The image of Serena in her bra and panties was still fresh in his mind.

"Satisfied?" Serena asked.

Marty looked up, startled. Could she read minds or something? "What?"

"About the wires? You good?"

"Oh." Marty thought for a second. Then he said, "I'm good. It's all good."

"Then let's talk," Serena said. She looked around the assembled group. "Let's talk about how we're going to kill Tanner-goddamn-Fritz."

Chapter Six

Carson

Carson leaned back, still stinging from Serena's basketball crack. He draped his arm along the top of the couch, knowing it encroached on Marty's space and made the smaller man nervous. If he was being honest, he liked making the accountant nervous. When Marty was nervous, he was an easy target to tease. He lost any and all ability to manufacture decent comebacks. Essentially, he became an insult punching bag. And Carson saw the entertainment and training value in bag work.

Marty scooted over, frowning sidewise at him.

Carson shrugged. No big deal. All he had to do to get Marty frazzled again was remind him he'd had sex with Serena. Then it'd be poor little puppy dog time again.

Serena was looking at him with an expectant frown. "Well?"

"What?" Carson asked, suddenly chastened. He pulled his arm off the top of the couch and dropped it into his lap. What was with her? She was up in his shit tonight.

"Wasn't this your idea to start with?" she asked. Her tone suggested that some blame needed to be assigned.

"No," he said automatically. "It was Stitch."

"No, it was you," Marty snapped back.

"Don't lie," Carson said. "It was totally your idea."

"You suggested it. We were at the bar and *you* suggested it."

Carson shook his head. "For the record, it was absolutely you." He looked at Serena. "It was him."

"I think it was a great idea," Serena said.

"It was my idea," Carson replied immediately. He glanced at Marty, who was shooting him the stink eye. "What? You were right. It was one hundred percent my brilliant idea."

Marty rolled his eyes. Carson thought about smacking him behind the head to fix that.

"The important thing," Serena was saying, "is that we all agree it's a good idea. Do we?"

"Of course," Carson said.

Barry didn't respond, but Carson couldn't tell with him if that meant he agreed or not.

Marty nodded. "I mean, yeah. We took off our clothes and everything, right?"

Carson was starting to wonder about both Marty and Barry now. Marty sounded wishy-washy and Barry was non-committal. Plus he had that head injury. Maybe this would end up being him and Serena, after all. Not that he'd mind.

Serena smiled slightly. Then she turned up her hands. "So if everyone is in, the question is, who gets to kill him?"

All three men shot their hands into the air. After a beat, Serena added her own.

So much for wondering about the other two. Of

course, Serena had a way of convincing people to do what she wanted.

The foursome looked around at one another for a few moments. Then Carson realized their predicament. Only one person could do the deed.

"It should be me," Carson quickly said.

Serena lowered her arm. The others followed suit. "Why you?" she asked.

"It was my idea. I get, like, the copyright or something."

"It's not a pop song," Marty scoffed. "You can't copyright an idea."

"Oh yeah? What about flight, huh? The Wright Brothers copyrighted that idea."

"No, they didn't. They got a *patent* on a plane design, not the idea of flight. You can't copyright an idea, or patent it, or trademark it. At least, not a general concept like, oh, I don't know . . . killing someone?"

"Then I call dibs," Carson said.

"N-n-no dibs on m-m-murder," Barry said.

"You said there was no rule book, Barry!"

"D-dibs on m-m-murder is s-s-stupid."

"Your face is stupid."

Serena held up her hands. "Enough!" She waited for the three of them to turn their attention to her, then said, "Carson has a point."

Carson raised his arms in triumph. "Woo-hoo! See, boys? Listen to the smart one."

"Then again," Serena continued, "maybe there's a better way to go about this."

Carson lowered his arms with a dejected frown. He could never seem to get a solid handle on Serena.

Was she on his side, or not? Did she dig him, or just use him for the occasional bang?

Serena is an enema, he thought.

No, that wasn't the right word. He couldn't think of what the right word was, but he knew there was one. It meant mysterious or hard to figure out.

Eczema? Something like that.

"What better way?" he asked her, suspicious.

"We all have a beef with him," she explained. "Serious ones. So shouldn't we should all work together to kill him?"

Carson considered her proposal, looking for the trap in it. He knew Serena was smarter than him in most ways, so he had developed a healthy caution where she was concerned. He heard both Marty and Barry parrot their approval while he thought it over.

Then he saw the catch.

"Fine with me," he said. "But no matter how much we work together, one thing is true: unless we're going to stand around him with knives and all stab him at the same time, it's going to be one single person that does the deed."

"He's right," Marty said. He sounded reluctant to agree with Carson, and a little aggrieved. But that was classic Marty. "I'm not feeling the whole Caesar vibe."

Caesar? What the hell does salad have to do with this? Carson thought for a moment, and decided the metaphor must mean because a Caesar is all tossed together, just like it would be if all of them killed Tanner together. Then he thought about a funny joke he'd heard about tossing someone's salad.

"What's so funny?" Serena asked.

Maybe I'll show you later. "Nothing." He looked around at his friends. "Everyone can help me, but I get to be the one to kill him. Agreed?"

No one answered.

"*Agreed?*" he tried again. He gave each one of them a look that he hoped would convince them. Threatening for Marty, placid for Barry, and sexy for Serena. He figured that would work for at least two out of three, maybe all three.

"No," said Marty.

"N-no," said Barry.

"No," said Serena.

Well, fuck.

Carson threw up his hands. "What's your bright idea, then? Because someone has to do it. Why not me?"

"Why not any of us?" Marty asked.

"Because it was *my* idea." Carson tapped his temple. "Copyright, remember?"

"You can't—"

"Guys." Serena's voice was low, but it stopped them both. Carson knew the tone well. She brought it out when play time was over. "We're going to be fair about this."

"Fair how?" Marty asked her.

"How about this? Whoever Tanner has screwed over the worst is the one who gets to kill him," she announced. "His worst victim makes the plan and gets to drop the hammer on him." She met each of their gazes in turn. "Yeah?"

The silence that followed was short. Then Barry mumbled his agreement, followed by Marty. Serena turned to Carson.

Carson shrugged. "It doesn't matter. It's still me."

"You think he did *you* the worst?"

"Absolutely."

Marty groaned and Barry shook his head.

"How do you figure?" Serena asked him.

A spike of anger stoked in his chest. He held out a finger. "He stole the company from me. He bought me out for pennies on the dollar compared to what he sold it for. He ruined my financial life."

"Bullshit," Marty said. "You're doing fine at the dealership."

Carson brushed that comment away, not wanting to get into it. "The point is, I'm selling cars!" he snapped. "I was a big shot at an up-and-coming company that sold out to a company that was already up and had come."

Marty gave him a confused look. "What? That makes no sense."

"He stole millions from me!" Carson yelled.

"He stole my *wife*," Marty said.

"So what? Half the world is filled with women, Marty. Half the world isn't filled with my career."

Marty's look of confusion intensified. "Wait, are you saying your money is more important than a person?"

"Than a wife, yeah."

"You son of a—"

"He t-t-took me," Barry said sharply.

Both men stopped short, turning to Barry.

"Yeah, buddy," Carson said. "He took all of us for something. He's an asshole. That's why we're arguing over who gets to kill him."

"No," Barry insisted. "He took *me*." For

emphasis, he tapped his forehead.

"Oh." Carson said. Then, he added, "Shit."

Dude had a point, he had to admit. And that wasn't good.

"I'm sorry," Marty whispered. "I mean, you're right, he—"

Carson saw his advantage slipping away, so he jumped in. "But at least you still have your *job*, Barry. He didn't take that away." He could feel Marty and Serena staring at him in disbelief. He forged on. "I mean, it's a good job, right?"

Barry glared at him. His jaw twitched like he wanted to say something, but nothing came out right away. Carson had noticed that Barry had trouble forming sentences when he got angry. He imagined that was pretty frustrating, especially since he knew that if he'd had *his* brains bashed in to the point of being half a retard, he'd be pretty angry all the time.

"F-f-fuck you, Car-car-son," Barry sputtered.

"I'm just sayin'."

"Shut up, Carson," Serena said in that same low tone. She looked around at the three of them. "Clearly, we have a problem here. Everyone thinks their reason for killing Tanner is the most deserving."

"What about you?" Carson asked. "Why do you want to kill him?"

"None of your business. Fuck off."

Carson looked back to the other two. "Well, then that's it. She's out. One of the three of us gets to do it. And since it was my idea and my copyright, then I get—"

"Random," Barry said.

Carson stopped. "This is *not* random. It's right on point. We're talking about offing Tanner, and who should do it." He jerked a thumb toward his chest. "Which is me."

"No. How w-w-we decide. It should be r-r-random."

"It should be *me*," Carson insisted.

"I'll go with random," Marty agreed.

"Me, too," said Serena.

"You don't get a vote," Carson said, pointing at her.

She smiled coldly. "I'm in this. I get a vote. But since you've got your panties all wadded up, I'll step aside. It'll be decided randomly between the three of you who gets to do the deed."

Carson looked at her, trying to find the trap again. This time, though, he couldn't see one. "Okay, how?"

"Comp-p-puterized randomization algorithm," Barry said immediately.

"No way," Carson and Marty said at almost the same time. They looked at each other, and Carson waved for Marty to speak. He didn't have a specific reason himself, but had objected strictly on principle.

"Too easy for you to rig it," Marty explained.

"Yeah," Carson said, nodding and pointing. "That's exactly what I was thinking."

"I don't ch-ch-cheat," Barry said.

"Right," Carson replied, his sarcasm plain. "I'm sure you don't."

It was quiet for a moment. Carson was about to suggest a racquetball playoff for the honors when Marty spoke up.

"We'll draw straws," he said, and pointed to Serena. "She'll hold them."

Carson wasn't sure how he felt about that. On one hand, having Serena hold the straws could be a huge advantage for him. On the other, it could be none at all. Or she might even play it straight. He could never tell with her. If she did play it straight, he had a pretty poor shot at winning. He decided he didn't like the idea.

"I agree," Barry said.

"Me, too," said Serena.

Carson thought about pointing out that they'd already established that she didn't get a vote, but he didn't want to jeopardize the possibility that she'd do him a solid and rig the draw in his favor.

He flashed his best devil-may-care grin at Serena. "Let's do it," he said, giving her a little bit of the low, sexy rumble in his voice to go along with the wattage of his smile.

If *that* didn't work, nothing would.

Serena went to fashion the straws from toothpicks in his kitchen. Carson leaned back confidently and waited.

Five minutes later, he sat on the corner of the couch, his arms crossed in a sulk. "That was bullshit," he grumbled. "Completely rigged."

"It was fair and square," Marty said.

"It was *un*fair and...and..." he floundered for the opposite of square. Finally, he said, "*Un*square."

At the end of the couch, Barry sat, spinning the short straw jerkily between his thumb and forefinger. His expression was difficult to read, though Carson thought he saw a certain smugness

there.
, Dick.
"So," Serena said. "It's your show, Barry. What's the plan?"

Chapter Seven

Barry

Barry didn't like stress, especially since life had become so difficult for him. Just the day-to-day routine, the stuff most took for granted was as much as he liked to handle, no aggravation, no problems, and no kill-plan.

I should've th-th-thought it over, he brooded on the long walk home. His place was a solid four miles from Carson's apartment. The sky looked dark and he had hoped the rain would hold off but it didn't. He took advantage of rooftop overhangs when he could, hugging the sides of the building he passed along the way.

Why did I want it so badly?

He chastised himself every step along the way, berating himself for having leapt in without thinking. "K-k-kill Tanner. Sure, p-p-piece of cake."

The sky opened up, drenching him. He was only halfway home and dashed for the overhang on the nearby building.

Idiot, he thought as he ran. *Fucking idiot!*

He recognized the diner. It was sort of a fixture, a throwback, the kind of place that was straight out of the 1950s. He'd seen the sign a few times over the years and had always intended to give it a try. Inside, the counters were laminated with Formica. The stools were chrome-based mushrooms with red vinyl cushions, the kind that swiveled three hundred-sixty degrees. He dried his face and hair with his shirtsleeve and took a seat at the counter as far from anyone else as he could manage.

"Menu, hon," the waitress said. She was a blonde in jeans with a T-shirt bearing the diner's name—*Tom's Place: Eat here and get gas.* She slid a laminated menu onto the counter in front of him. Rain dripped from his hair onto the peeling countercard. The special of the day was meatloaf. "You got caught in the downpour, huh?" She handed him a wad of paper napkins. "Here you, go, sweetie."

"T-thanks." He dried his face thoroughly before running them over his hair. He balled up the wet napkins and placed them on the counter. "I'm m-m-more nervous than hungry."

"What are you so nervous about, sweetums?"

Barry felt his guts churning, the deep, dark secret eating away at him and pricking at his nerves. "W-w-work stuff," he said. "I've got p-problems at w-w-work."

"It's only a job, baby." She patted his hand. "You think the company you work for has some kind of exclusive on jobs? You don't like this one, start looking for another."

"G-g-good idea."

"You listen to old Lena, I'll learn ya." She was thin, in her forties, a good ten years older than him and somewhat motherly. "Just ain't worth the worry, am I right? What is it they say? Something about how worrying won't stop the bad stuff from happening, just stops you from enjoying the good." She gave him a wink. "Now, what can I get you?"

He pointed to the special. "I'll have the meatloaf, o-okay?"

"Sure, hon. It's *good*. Comes with two sides, soup or side salad. Chef just made a fresh batch of cream of potato and it's *deeee-lish*." She found the options on the menu and pointed to the list of sides. "We're out of the baked sweet potatoes but everything else is just fine. Stay away from the string beans, though. They're canned."

"Ok-k-kay, I'll have the soup."

She lit up. "The potato?"

"Y-yeah."

"You'll like it. Sides?"

"F-f-fries and creamed spinach?"

"Good choices." She handed him a copy of the local newspaper. "I'll put your order right in for you. Something to drink?"

"C-c-coffee."

"Coffee won't help you with that nervous condition of yours. How about a nice cup of herbal tea?"

He wrinkled his nose. "Just water."

He reached for the newspaper, hoping to distract himself, but it looked as if it had been read by everyone in town. The front page was food-stained and randomly saturated with spots of grease—not exactly what he wanted to touch before putting food in his mouth.

Lena placed a glass of water in front of him along with a plate of coleslaw and pickles. "Soup will be right up, hon."

"T-t-thanks."

"You always had that stutter?"

"Nuh-no. Work accident. M-my boss was too ch-ch-cheap to do things the right way. Equipment fell on me."

"Oh, no." Her concern sounded genuine.

Hot tears of anger sprang to Barry's eyes. "The b-b-bastard. His fault. M-made me a joke." He began to tremble the moment the words left his mouth. *I'm an idiot*, he thought. *I just spilled the beans. If the police question her they'll know I had motive. Stupid.*

It was almost impossible for him to meet her gaze but he finally found the courage and what he saw in her eyes startled him. She was furious, her eyes strained, red and veiny, her skin flush.

"Why, that sorry sack of shit. If someone screwed me over like that I'd want them dead, fucking dead." She picked up the tinny fork and bent it in her hand.

Barry's eyes grew large.

She rubbed his arm. "Poor baby. No wonder you're all shook up—you've got all that anger built up inside. You look like you're about to blow."

Two dings from the call bell turned her head. "Soups up," the cook said with a look of impatience. "Getting cold, Lena."

She turned away and didn't look up until she placed the cup of soup on the counter. When she did the fury had melted away and was completely gone. It was as if she had flipped a switch. She played with his finger as her face became alight with a smile.

"Say, hon, you seeing anyone?"

Barry couldn't finish his food. He didn't know if he was simply overwhelmed or having a stroke. There hadn't been any women in his life since his wife left him after the accident. Never so much as a serious display of affection, outside of Serena's friendly gestures. The computer server accident had rendered him a joke, a prostrate joke of a man incapable of happiness.

"So, you've been . . . *off* since the accident?" Lena asked. They'd moved from the counter to a booth in the back of the diner. It was around a corner and tucked in at the end by the closet where the cleaning supplies were kept. Barry could smell the powerful odor of bleach seeping from behind the closet door and imagined most patrons would refuse to sit there voluntarily.

"Y-y--you're boss isn't going to get-get mad at you sitting here with me?" he asked.

"I told him I'm on my break. He don't like it, it's just too damn bad. Place ain't exactly hopping, now is it?"

Barry looked around. "No."

"You feeling any better? I can bring you some ginger ale—a good belch fix you right up."

"No, I'm g-g-good. I've just got a lot, a lot on my mind."

She flicked his finger with hers. "What's going on in there?"

What's going on here? he wondered. *Why is she coming on so strong?* He couldn't understand her interest in him but enjoyed it all the same. "A lot on my m-m-mind. A lot of p-p-pressure." He became quiet. It had been such a long time since he'd spent time with any woman other than Serena, and in his mind she was like one of the guys. "I used to be m-m-married," he told Lena, "but no more."

"Your wife left you?"

He nodded, his expression pathetic. "Y-yes."

"Because of the accident?"

He repeated the same sad nod.

"Well, that woman ain't worth a pile of shit. What kind of gal gives up on her man when he's down?" She stood abruptly. "Be right back. You ain't gonna leave are you?"

Barry shook his head. "No. I'll w-w-wait."

Lena returned in a flash. She set down a mug and pulled a pint of Bushmill's from the pocket of her apron. She poured a shot into his cup. "Water of life," she said. "Fix you right up."

"Water of life?"

"It's what whiskey means. It's an old Gaelic term."

He pondered the information for a moment, then lifted the mug and imbibed the doctor's prescription. It was getting late. Outside the traffic had grown sparse. He set down the mug and smiled as a pleasant numbness spread across his head.

"How about we exchange phone numbers?" she said. "Don't take this the wrong way but I think you need some company."

Is this pity or something worse? What does she want with me?

"Take out your phone," she directed. "I'll give you my number and you can give me yours."

"Y-y-you're . . ." He was going to say aggressive but was able to rein it in. "Direct."

"Sorry," she said. "My boss is giving me the stink eye. I just figured . . .?"

He took out his phone and handed it to her. She punched in her number and pressed send. Her phone lit up and buzzed.

"Done," she said. "Do you remember my name, hon?"

"Lena, r-r-right?"

"That's right, hon, Lena. Lena Pretty." She tapped his phone screen. "Here, I'll save it for you."

The sound of a powerful car rumbled out on the street. The window began to vibrate in time with the exhaust burble. Lena checked her watch. "Five, four, three, two..."

Tanner's yellow Lamborghini flashed by.

"Right on schedule," Lena said.

Barry saw the vehicle and his boss' profile as the sports car shot through the intersection, pulling to the curb in front of a pub. "Right on skuh-skuh-schedule? W-what do you mean?"

"The yellow menace over there hits the bar every week about this time—some slick-looking dude and his K-girlfriend."

"What's a K-k-*k* girlfriend?"

"His Korean chippy. Tall, dresses like a runway model, big bolt-on titties. Byrne—he owns the place—keeps it dark so men can take their secret gal pals there. It's upscale and quiet. Can't say parking the yellow menace out front is a good idea, though. Not too many screaming yellow Lambos in this neck of the woods."

Barry watched as Tanner got out of the car, then walked around the back to the other side and offered a hand to a leggy woman getting out of the car. *Son of a bitch—goddamn Tanner is everywhere I turn.* An idea began to take shape in his mind, and he focused on it. He manipulated his thoughts with the same alacrity he solved coding problems: analyzing, ordering, and reordering lines of code until everything made perfect sense.

"Hey, earth to Barry. You in there, hon? You've got this silly expression on your face." She waved her hand in front of his face but he didn't flinch. "You all right? That whiskey mess you up or something?"

He was in his head, hunkered down, planning, plotting, scheming, and for the moment happier than he had been in a long while.

"Shoot," she said. "I think the hooch done messed you up. Why didn't you tell me you can't hold your liquor?"

She sounded nervous and panicky. Her concern gladdened him. He reached out and took her hand. A huge grin spread across his face and he spoke in a clear deliberate tone, "No worries. I'm *good*."

Chapter Eight

Serena

Where Asian noodles were concerned, Serena was a chow fun kind of girl. She liked her rice noodles soft and wide—the wider the better, chewy and comforting.

She sat at one of three small tables that were lined up against the window of the Chinese takeout place across the street from the 1950s-style diner. There was no way to hear what Barry and the floozy waitress were saying but that didn't matter. Their body language spoke volumes.

She'd trailed him from Carson's apartment after their meeting, all the while the question she had asked looping in her head.

It's your show, Barry. What's the plan?

She knew he didn't have one. He was as much an amateur as the other two and maybe worse off because it wasn't in him to be vindictive.

She watched him every step of the way as he ambled down the street going in the general direction of his apartment taking an occasional wrong turn, turns that surprised her. It was as if he was somewhat sure of where he lived but not one hundred percent, as if he'd moved recently and hadn't entirely committed the route to memory.

No Dibs On Murder

He's completely fucked up, she thought. *He's so nervous about committing murder he doesn't know where he's going. Better keep an eye on the poor schmuck before he wanders into the wrong part of town and gets jacked up.*

She was surprised when he yanked on the diner door and went in. She figured he must be fried and needed to sit down to collect his thoughts.

She ducked into the Chinese restaurant when she saw him looking at the menu. She ordered quickly all the while keeping an eye on Barry. The especially attentive crone waitress struck her as particularly interesting.

Serena plunged the chopsticks into the large bowl of rice noodles and mashed them between her molars. *What are the chances he gets the nod to kill Tanner and gets lucky all in the same day?*

She didn't have her full-size SLR Nikon with her. The iPhone would have to do. She snapped long-range shots with one hand while continuing to shovel noodles into her mouth with the other.

"Who is this chick?" she muttered between bites. She'd certainly find out. Now that she knew where the woman worked and what she looked like, she could do some investigating. For starters, she'd walk in when the woman was off duty and inquire discreetly. Then, with her resources and experience, the rest would be a piece of cake.

Not that Barry didn't deserve the affections of a woman, but he was after all, Barry—a stumbling, bumbling former shadow of himself, a man who by his own admission hadn't been with a woman since his wife left him. Serena wondered for a moment if she should have thrown some pity sex his way, but realized those days were long past. No confidence meant no turn-on for her.

The thing was, she hadn't worried about this lack of confidence when she drew him into the conspiracy. Despite his injury, Barry had certain skills that they might need. Besides, he deserved a shot. Tanner Fritz stole his brains, after all.

Serena grinned around her mouthful of noodles while she watched Barry and the waitress do the flirtation dance. The four of them were a murderous version of *The Wizard of Oz*. Tanner was some reverse incarnation of the Wizard, stealing gifts instead of bestowing them. In a manner of speaking, Barry had the Scarecrow's brains. Marty fit neatly into the role of the Tin Man, his heart stolen away when his wife, Andrea left.

What about Carson, though? The Cowardly Lion didn't want money, but courage. Maybe she'd have to find another way to shoehorn Carson into this analogy. But after a few moments of thought, she realized he actually fit the Cowardly Lion perfectly. He may have thought that Tanner took his money, but she saw that what he really stole was Carson's confidence.

And here I thought my psychology degree would be wasted in HR.

So who did that make her? Dorothy, wanting to go home?

She snorted at the thought, surprised she didn't shoot jasmine tea out her nostrils.

Dorothy? Hardly.

She went back to watching the waitress talking to

Barry. The woman had to be a living, breathing loon, a complete wacko. Meanwhile, there was Barry, suddenly fluid in the art of conversation, chatting up a sure thing. The idea seemed ludicrous, but there it was, happening right across the street from her.

Serena finished the noodles, then looked down at the wrapped fortune cookie that sat on the table in front of her. She hated the taste of the maple-flavored cookies but wasn't going to pass up the fortune that waited within. She smashed the package with the side of her hand and pulled the clear cellophane bag apart. Foraging through the cookie crumbs she found the white slip of paper and held it open with her thumbs and forefingers.

Love is a winged butterfly that fears the net.

She scrunched her brow. That read like nonsense at first. Then she thought about poor Marty and how he lost Andrea. It wasn't a perfect fit, but that didn't matter.

She let her mind drift while she watched the pair across the street. The fortune referencing butterflies and nets reminded her of how collecting such insects and impaling them on a board for display used to be a huge pastime in high society. Was it still? She wondered about that. With the advent of electronics, her guess was probably not. But there still had to be people in the world who collected specimens, even if their numbers had dwindled. In any case, she certainly understood the inclination.

The camera was still trained on Barry and the waitress when a streak of yellow flashed in front of the lens, breaking her reverie. She followed the blur and saw Tanner's Lamborghini pulling to the curb further down the block. Tanner got out of the car, and took a leggy Asian girl by the arm before he swaggered toward the bar, laughing as they entered.

"Now what?" *This just keeps getting better and better.*

As much as she wanted to follow Barry to see if he went home with the slutty hag, he had just dropped to the second rung on the ladder. She left the restaurant and found a coffee shop down the block where she could kill time and wait for Tanner and his date to emerge.

She thought about Andrea. They'd been friends since right after college and had been really close throughout her marriage to Marty, but when she left him for Tanner . . . well, Serena judged traitors harshly. Sure, Marty whined a lot. He'd been insanely jealous of her, while at the same time spending too much time either at work or watching sci-fi movies. Serena was sure all of it was born out of his own insecurity, but it was no wonder that Andrea eventually became distant. In the end, she figured, Marty was so convinced that he'd married above his station that he managed to convince her of it, too. Yet, for all his faults, he didn't deserve the screwing over he got, and definitely not in the way he got it. After that happened, Andrea was shit in Serena's eye.

"I'm going to take a whole lot of pictures," she said quietly, her voice disappearing with the wind as she exited the restaurant. "And if I get a shot of this whore sitting on Tanner's face . . . Andrea will be the first to see it."

Chapter Nine

Carson

"You won't find a better vehicle on the market," Carson told his customer. "Not unless you're willing to pay twice as much, and even then, you'd get an inferior product."

The man he was trying to sell wore casual slacks and a silk shirt that was open at the collar. A thick gold chain hung at this throat, and Carson had noted the opulent rings he wore on both hands. Some people might think the look was loud, signifying new or ill-gained money, but he saw it differently.

He saw a guy who liked to spend and show.

Carson respected that. After all, what was the point of having money if you didn't spend it? If you go to all the work of being a winner and earning it, you should show the world what you've accomplished. That's how he lived, and if he'd made the millions he should have made when Santo Corp bought out Chismo . . .

"You're saying this is better than a Mercedes?"

Carson ground his teeth, more at the thought of his lost fortune than the question, and forced himself to smile. "Mercedes is fine for Europe," he said, "and if you want the truth, there were a few years there that those Germans had us on the run. But we

Americans learn fast. We adapt. We scrap. You look like the kind of American who knows exactly what I mean."

He actually looked like the kind of American who made his money on the dark side of the law, which Carson supposed was somewhat the same thing. The guy wasn't as seedy as Carson's sports bookie, but he could have easily been a tier or two higher in *La Famiglia*.

The man gave him a dubious look. Carson had seen this game face plenty of times. The customer wanted to push for the best deal he could. They all did. That was fine. The sticker price gave him a little room to maneuver.

"Tell you what," he said, wanting to close this one. He really needed the sale. Besides that, he was supposed to meet Marty for lunch. "The manager is away at a sales conference this week, so I have full authority on all my sales. I'll take three thousand off the manufacturer's price, just for you. That's the manufacturer's price, not the sticker price." He pointed at the sticker in the window of the model with its wildly inflated price for emphasis. The manufacturer's price wasn't listed, but that never seemed to matter. Either the customer's imagination filled one in, or he'd provide it when asked. It wasn't like it was the real number anyway, just one Carson pulled out of his ass to make the customer feel like he was getting the best possible deal.

The man pulled out a phone and started scrolling. Carson clenched his jaw. This usually meant trouble. He considered saying something to break the man's concentration, but held back. It would only make things worse. So, he waited, a slow dread collecting in his gut.

"Mmmm," the man finally said. Then he nodded to himself, and turned the phone toward Carson. He read the number, which was significantly lower than the deal he'd just offered. "This is the average dealer price, according to CarTrue."

Carson gave him his best smile. "That's not actually an accurate website," he tried to explain, even though he knew better. "It's not averaged. They base that price on the absolute least expensive model, with no options. Not even floor mats."

He broadened his smile, as if to say *can you believe that shit?* The man didn't so much as blink.

Carson pressed on. "And I think they use Arkansas or someplace like that with a much lower cost-of-living than here. I can't match that price."

"I don't want that price," the customer said.

That was encouraging, at least. Now he had some room to operate. "I knew you were a reasonable guy when you walked in here," he said.

"I want one thousand below this price," the man said, tapping his phone.

Carson's face fell. "I... I can't do that." The truth was he could, but just barely. His commission would be so minimal it wouldn't be worth the paperwork.

"Then I guess I'll go down the street to Howe's, and see what they can do for me there."

You prick.

The customer was already walking toward the door. Carson stared after him for a couple of beats before scrambling to catch up. "Wait," he said, hating the tone in his voice. "I think we can work something out."

The man slowed but didn't stop. He held up his phone. "CarTrue doesn't lie. Apparently you do."

"I didn't lie to you," Carson said.

The man jabbed the phone toward him, causing Carson to flinch. Then, without a word, he turned and left the dealership.

Carson considered going after him again. He might be able to talk the man back inside. Hell, he could even whittle the price down to virtually no commission if he had to, just to get the stat. If he didn't bump those up, his manager would be on his ass again.

But the confident stride of the man walking away made him think of Tanner Fritz, and that made him angry all over again. He wouldn't have to kowtow to these smart-phone-wielding wiseasses if Tanner hadn't cheated him.

He let the son of a bitch walk.

Carson watched until the man got into his car and drove away. Then he turned to see if anyone had seen his failure. Luckily, most people were already at lunch or with other customers.

He spotted Alice still at her desk. She sat erect in her chair, clicking furiously at her keyboard. Her therapy retriever lay at her feet, a black service vest standing out against its golden fur.

"Alice!" Carson said, approaching her.

She jumped in her seat. The dog rose to a sitting position. When she turned, her expression was harried. Then she saw Carson, and her cheeks reddened slightly.

He knew the mousey girl had a crush on him. It

had been that way his whole life. Women gravitated to him like he was a movie star. Many of them were way hotter than Alice. He'd gotten used to it, even took it for granted. Most of the time, it worked to his advantage.

"Yes?" Alice asked, pushing her glasses back. "How can you help me?"

When she realized what she'd said, her face blossomed fully red in embarrassment.

Carson smiled benevolently, ignoring her mistake. "I'm going to go to lunch, but would you do me a small favor?" He squatted down and scratched the golden retriever on the head.

Alice frowned. "You're not supposed to touch a service animal," she informed him. "Not when they're working."

Carson removed his hand. "Sorry, I always forget. He's such a handsome guy."

"*Her* name's Merlot," Alice muttered.

"A pretty name for a pretty girl," Carson said. "Anyway, I'm headed to lunch, but if you see any good prospects roll in, I need you to text me, all right?"

Alice considered. There was a specific protocol for walk-ins and he was asking her to bypass it. "I don't know…"

He flashed a high-wattage smile. "I'd really appreciate it."

"Well… I suppose this once –"

"Great!" With that settled, he rose and headed for the door. He was late to lunch.

Marty was already there when he arrived. He was drinking a beer, which wasn't his normal lunch fare.

"You started without me."

"You're late."

Carson grunted and settled into the high-backed stool. He waved at the waitress, pointing to Marty's glass.

"Liquid lunch?" Marty asked, a little surprised. "Won't your customers smell it on your breath?"

Carson shrugged. "If I go back, I'll chew some mints."

"*If* you go back?"

Carson shrugged. "There's no action. If this keeps up, I'll get bumped over to the used car lot by the end of the month."

Marty looked concerned. "Is money still tight? I thought that after the bankruptcy—"

Carson waved his words away, hoping no one overheard. Marty had really come through earlier in the year, walking him through the process when he needed some reorganizing with his finances, but the rest of the world didn't need to know that. "It's not my fault. The market's down. People just don't seem to understand what a new car has to offer like they once did."

Marty's look of concern lessened, but only a little. "You'd be better off. A new car is such a poor investment. You lose money as soon as you drive off the lot."

"Still better than buying used."

"No," Marty said. "A used car is the smartest way to go. About three years old with low miles. That's the best bargain. You could really sell that idea to people, Carson. I know you could."

Carson shook his head. "A three-year old car doesn't come with that new car smell. It comes with someone else's stink in it."

"They make air fresheners with new car scent."

"It's not the same. Besides, you're buying more than a new car when you get one of ours. You're buying *status*."

"And exactly where does status show up on a balance sheet?"

"Status is the kind of thing that helps you close even bigger deals. It affects the bottom line, trust me." He saw Marty's doubtful expression, so he tried to explain. "You ride with a realtor, do you want to ride in one of my products or a three-year-old Yugo? Status matters."

"If I'm buying a house, why do I care what kind of car the realtor drives?"

Carson sighed. "Look, it's like leadership on a sports team, an intangible. But it matters."

"Were you betting on intangibles when you lost big on last week's game?"

Carson's eyes narrowed in a scowl. "How'd you know about that?"

Marty took a swig of his beer, looking smugly superior. Carson's beer arrived, and the waitress waited expectantly for their meal order. Both settled on the special. When she'd walked away, Carson repeated his question.

"Seriously, Marty, how'd you know?"

"Come on. I've known you since forever. I can tell when you win big, and I can tell when you lose big. You're all out of sorts. That's how you were last week, so I know you lost big." He eyed Carson knowingly. "Tell me I'm wrong."

Carson sighed. "It wasn't that much. I was just pissed because it was supposed to be a lock."

"The win or the points?"

"Doesn't matter." Carson took a swallow of his beer. "Jesus, you're a downer. Why am I even friends with you?"

"We've been friends since college. You're stuck with me."

"How do you figure?"

Marty cocked his head at him. "How many new friends have you made as a grown-up?"

"Lots. I'm a good guy. People love me."

"Ha!" Marty barked.

"What's so funny?"

Marty shook his head. "Never mind. The point is, you haven't made any friends since college. Not real ones."

Carson scowled at him. What the hell was Marty talking about? He had plenty of friends. He sipped his beer, considering what Marty meant by 'real friends.' The concept slowly took hold. Did he know anyone he could have even joked about the Tanner situation with, much less actually following through?

Damn, he thought. *He's right.*

"See?" Marty said. "I'm right."

"No, you're not."

Marty raised his eyebrows, then took another drink of his beer.

Carson let the idea sink in. "Jesus," he muttered. "It's like a goddamn prison sentence, when you think about it."

They mumbled about trivial matters until their food came. Carson had been hungry when he arrived, but their downer conversation had curbed his appetite. Now, the smell of the onion rings brought it raging back, and he tore into his lunch.

"You know what's bullshit?" he said around a mouthful of his sandwich.

"That they charge dinner prices for a sourdough melt?"

"That, too." Carson swallowed his food. "But I'm talking about Barry. Why should he get to do the deed?"

Marty looked stricken. He stopped chewing and looked around furtively to see if anyone heard. "I...I don't think we should be talking about this here." He thought for a second, and added, "Or anywhere."

Carson waved his comment away. "Nobody knows what we're talking about."

"Not now, maybe. But if someone is listening, and then thinks about it after..." he trailed off, giving Carson a beseeching look.

"Don't be a nancy."

"Lower your voice."

"No one can hear us."

"They won't if you lower your voice."

"Oh, my God." Carson peered at him closely. "Is it hard to be such a scared little hamster all the time, Marty?"

"I'm just being smart."

"That's what you call it?" He shook his head and took a huge bite of his sandwich. He glared at Marty while he chewed and swallowed. "I'm worried about you," he said.

"Me?"

"Yeah, you. You go around looking like a basket case, and someone is going to get suspicious. You have to act like everything is normal."

"I am!"

Carson thought about it, then shrugged. Maybe that was true. Marty always was a bit of a nerve case.

"Whatever," he said. "That wasn't my point, anyway. My point is that Barry getting the call is bullshit."

"He won the draw, fair and square."

"No, it wasn't fair. Or square."

"Huh?"

"It's a stupid way to decide. All that Barry is going to do is screw it up and get caught. And then who's to say he doesn't give us all up to the cops to save his own disabled ass?"

Marty's stricken look deepened. "You don't think he'd do that, do you?"

Carson sighed. "No. I don't suppose he would. Or Serena, either. She's stone cold unbreakable."

"What about me?"

"I think you'd crack under interrogation."

"No, I wouldn't." Marty was indignant. "I'd never sell out my friends."

"I don't think you'd want to, but…" Carson held up his hand and waggled it. "You'd get nervous, and spill."

"What about you? If it was your ass on the line, you'd give up all three of us in an instant to save it."

"Oh, come on."

"You know it's true. You're selfish, Carson."

Carson pretended to consider. Then he said, "With my bargaining skills, I don't think I'd need to give up all three of you. I could talk them into letting me just give them just one—*you*."

Marty blanched, and put his sandwich down.

Carson laughed. "Oh, relax, Marty. I'd never do that. Especially not to you."

"Sure, you wouldn't." Marty's tone was dubious.

"I'm serious." The truth was that if it came down to it, he probably would but he knew the lie made Marty feel better. "You're my best friend. If I gave you up and they sent you away, what would I do? Like you said, it's not like I can make any new friends."

His words seemed to placate Marty, who picked up his sandwich and began eating again.

"I still say it's bullshit, though," Carson said. "Barry's the last of us that should get the nod."

"You don't think he deserves it?"

"We all deserve it," Carson said. *And I deserve it the most.* "But he's the least likely to get the job done, and if he fails, then where are we?"

Marty thought about it. "I guess it'll be someone else's turn, right?"

Carson stopped chewing.

"What?" Marty said. "What's that look on your face?"

Carson didn't know what expression Marty saw, but he transformed it into a huge grin. "Marty, you're a genius."

"You say that every year when I do your taxes."

"I mean it this time." Carson put down his

sandwich and lifted his beer. "Here's to that stuttering fuck blowing it so one of us can get a kick at the can."

Marty stared at him a moment before understanding what Carson meant. Then he raised his own glass.

Carson clinked it and drank deeply. The beer tasted delicious. The sandwich was delicious. Yeah, things could be better at the car lot, but he was lucky enough to have been born Carson, and that was something to be grateful for. And now, there was a good chance he'd get an opportunity to take his revenge on Tanner-Goddamn-Fritz. All that he needed was for Barry to fail at his attempt.

And did he think that Barry would fail?

Oh, yes. He'd take those odds any day.

Chapter Ten

Barry

Barry walked into the diner where Lena worked not knowing what kind of greeting to expect but registered a small amount of self-confidence as he bellied up to the counter. He was feeling good about himself in a way he hadn't felt since before the accident, since before his life went to shit. He didn't see her at first but soon recognized her loud voice coming from the kitchen. It sounded as if she was busting the cook's chops. Barry assumed that she didn't abide mistakes where they impacted her tip money.

The kitchen door swung wide and she stepped forward. When she saw him, she smiled and planted both palms on the counter in front of him. "I guess you really like the goddamn meatloaf."

He was taken aback momentarily, his lips parting slightly, his breath frozen.

She winked at him and smacked him on the shoulder. "Lighten up, Barry. I know men—they've got two brains and neither is between the ears." She leaned forward, her face inappropriately close to his. "So what's it gonna be, you hungry or horny?"

"I-I-I . . ."

"Both it is. Except we only serve the meatloaf

every other day. Tuesday, Thursday, and Saturday it's Salisbury steak but if you smother the ground beef with ketchup it's so darn close to the meatloaf it's hard to tell the difference. Sometimes I don't bother to tell folks which is which, but seeing as we're amigos…" She pulled a heavily laminated menu from the counter stand, opened it, and placed it in front of him. "How do you feel about stuffed cabbage? Chopped meat-speaking, it's just another variation on the theme."

"C-cabbage makes me f-f-fart," he whispered.

"Speak up, hon. No need to whisper. Cabbage makes everyone fart." She went silent for a moment while she thought of alternatives. "Last option—I can dump in a can of baked beans on the Salisbury steak and make a hobo chili. Yes or no?"

"I'm not sure. Anyway, how-how are you?" he asked, his confidence evaporating like dog pee on a Miami sidewalk.

"I'm right as rain, sweetheart. Saw the gyno before work—my lady parts are A-okay. Got fitted for a new IUD too. Only thing is the damn thing needs an alignment—kind of pokes me in the hind parts every time I bend over. I'm kind of worried you might have a big pecker and give me some kind of internal bleeding."

He clasped his hand over his mouth to prevent a loud roar from filling the diner. This woman was unlike anyone he'd ever known.

And I like it.

Lena grabbed the menu and stuffed it back into the holder. "I'll look around back and see if we've got anything fresh." She spun around and disappeared through the swinging door.

Within thirty minutes Barry had eaten an enormous salad, a cup of broccoli-cheddar soup, and was soaking up sauce from his plate with a dinner roll.

"Can you believe it," Lena began, "I forgot about pastitsio? It's a Greek diner and I forget the goddamn Greek lasagna. If that don't beat all—why, that's like forgetting we serve baklava for dessert. Good, huh?"

Barry nodded and pushed the saturated bread into his mouth. He chewed thoroughly and swallowed. "You w-w-work every day?"

"Why you want to know? Planning on asking me on a date?"

He shrugged. "Think I s-s-should?"

"Look, honey, a man's got to make up his own mind. All I can say is that I've been dropping hints all over creation and I'm beginning to wonder about your sexual orientation. You dig va-jay-jay or don't you?"

Barry froze while lifting the last piece of bread toward his mouth. ". . . Can-can I walk you home?"

She put her chin down on crossed arms. "Well, ain't you sweet. I live clear across town, sugar, but you can walk me to the bus if you like. I get off in thirty."

Chapter Eleven

Serena

Serena's Nikon camera was digital but it still employed a mechanical SLR shutter and clicked loudly with every frame. Snap. Snap. Snap. She wasn't bashful with her digital exposures and had already taken close to thirty shots of Barry and the waitress. She could tell from their body language and the time she spent with him that there was more being discussed than food. She didn't remember Barry mentioning that he frequented the diner but assumed there was a lot about Barry he kept confidential.

She'd never considered photography as a hobby unto itself, but the camera served a vital purpose when she went on her antiquing trips. She'd come prepared with a second battery and high-volume data chip for the camera as well as a telephoto lens. She had a thermos of coffee filled with Starbuck's high octane in her bag. There was an app on her phone for dictation in case she wanted to take notes.

One thing Serena knew about herself was that she was meticulous. If she ever turned her analytical skills inward—and she had, on occasion—the result would be an admission that *meticulous* was a euphemism for borderline OCD. She preferred to think of it as *careful*. She lived a careful life, punctuated by risks, large and small, that she further mitigated by her meticulous nature. It was no accident, for instance, that her vehicle was black and blended in at night. She had parked it across the street from the diner where she could see but not be seen. Additionally, she had a checklist and had already ticked off some of the essential requirements of a quality surveil: the time and date the surveillance had begun, the location and notes on what she was witnessing.

Things plodded along inside the diner until the waitress came out from behind the counter carrying a shoulder bag. Through her high-resolution lens, Serena could see the huge grin on Barry's face. She watched as they exited the diner together and walked up the street. She changed the lens and quietly slipped out of the car. Slinging the camera strap around her neck, she hustled across the street a full block behind them. With the camera hanging at her waist, she continued to click off shots like an western gunslinger firing in rapid succession.

Babbling Barry isn't as helpless as he lets on, she thought. *But I already knew that. Good for him, though.*

She took another hip-shot photo of the pair.

Now, if only I could hear what they were saying.

She noted the way they walked, that slow crawl new acquaintances use when they're more interested in getting to know each other than reaching their destination. Their heads were turned toward each other, asking questions and receiving answers, smiling... flirting.

She glanced down at the camera and saw her data card was ninety-four percent full. That didn't surprise her. She had collected a treasure chest of snapshots, photos of Tanner Fritz and his Asian tart, as well as photos of Barry and the waitress who, she'd learned, went by the name Lena Pretty. She didn't need any more, but she took them nonetheless. *You never knew.* Sometimes she discovered things when looking at photographs later than she'd missed when she'd fired off the shot. Not often, but it was still a thrilling discovery when it happened.

Serena had dug into Ms. Pretty's background. The woman was Arkansas born and bred, three ex-husbands and no kids. *Something wrong there*, Serena thought. *Bad lady parts maybe.* She had shitty credit. Collection accounts. Hadn't filed a tax return in twelve years. She scored big when the governor's drunk baby brother rear-ended her at a Hot Springs stoplight late one night. That netted her a brand new Toyota Camry and fifty-K hush money.

Serena was adept at digging up dirt. Some of the methods she'd learned on her own, and some she'd gleaned from Barry. The irony of that didn't escape her now.

But Lena Pretty wasn't her only target. She'd need to get the lowdown on Tanner's cosmetically enhanced Asian bimbo, too. That woman came from money, though, and money insulates. She'd have to be cleverer to get the 411 on her but get it she would. And even with the tame rated PG pictures she's taken of her and Tanner... well, Mrs. Andrea Fritz was in for a rude-fucking-awakening.

Serena was hoping.

Served her right. Back in college, Serena had managed to wrap her friends around her little finger. Each one required a different approach. Carson was the easiest, though finding the right amount of push and pull to keep him on the line when he was at the height of his confidence took some finesse. Barry turned out to be the one with whom she could share just a little bit of her true self. Tanner, of course, was impregnable, but at the same time everyone's best friend, the glue that held the group together all the way through school and beyond. He was her Mt. Everest, but she was patient. She always figured that time would come, though now rather than sexual conquest, she'd find greater satisfaction in his demise.

And then there was Marty, sweet, hapless Marty, who Serena had a soft spot for even as she had groomed him. It was a years-long process with the goal of bringing him completely inside her circle once she know she could trust him unconditionally. Things were headed that way unerringly until... Andrea.

Not only did the bitch steal Marty away, but then she fucking broke him, leaving him useless for Serena's purposes. It was a double shot of betrayal, and for that, Andrea would face retribution.

She'd already thought about how she'd tell Tanner's wife. There was the anonymous route, of course — ring the doorbell and leave a nondescript yellow envelope for Andrea to find.

What's the fun in that, though?

She was leaning toward the concerned friend

approach—up close and personal, be there when her life ember was snuffed out. "We've been BFFs forever. I didn't want to tell you but . . ." She'd pause and mist up for effect. "I thought you had the right to know. I was sitting alone in a coffee shop when the yellow Lamborghini pulled up across the street from me and well, I think Tanner's ramming Asian twat. I mean, the girl is young and hot—huge porn-star boobs."

She envisioned Andrea getting sick in front of her. Andrea was a piss-poor drinker and Serena had been there for her before, holding her hair while she got cozy with the commode even though she wanted to strangle the man-thief with her own blonde mane. When sick like that, Andrea's normally rosy complexion quickly turned ashen white. She rarely wore waterproof makeup. Serena envisioned thick black lines snaking down over those all-too-perfect cheekbones.

Payback's a bitch, bitch!

Serena squirreled herself away, out of sight in a locksmith's doorway, while Barry and Ms. Arkansas waited at a bus stop. There was still plenty of eye contact between Barry and his trailer trash princess. It looked as if she was doing most of the talking and touched his arm frequently. Fifteen minutes passed, then twenty. Lena seemed to nod her head in agreement. Thanks to shitty city transit, it appeared they were going to forgo the bus ride in favor of a long and romantic stroll home.

Are they going to his house or hers?

Serena followed after them. Within a couple of blocks it was clear they weren't going to Barry's place.

Now I know why she takes the bus, Serena thought as her calves began to ache. Her loafers were perfect for the plush-carpeted office floors but they were now two miles from the diner and she could feel a blister forming between the toes of her right foot.

They eventually reached her house. Despite her worry about the wild card that Lena Pretty represented, she couldn't help but smile as Barry climbed the front steps and followed her inside.

"Good for you, tiger. Go get some."

Chapter Twelve

Marty

Bourbon wasn't Marty's thing.

It was Carson's thing, sure. And no doubt, Tanner drank the stuff. Probably looked elegant and suave and slick while he did so, like some dude on the cover of a cigar magazine.

Wait, Marty thought. *Why a cigar magazine? He's drinking Scotch.*

No, not Scotch. Bourbon.

Ah, shit. I'm drunk.

He hadn't intended to get drunk, or so he told himself. The idea was just to have one drink to take the edge off. There was a lot going on, and it was happening fast. It made him nervous and exhilarated him all at once.

Just one drink. That was the plan. And so that he'd go slow and sip it, he opted for the bourbon. He kept a bottle in the high cupboard above the fridge for emergencies, and it rarely made an appearance. The truth was, if Carson didn't come by, it would go untouched for months.

He thought of it as his quiet bottle and quiet bottles were made for sipping.

But Marty lied. He drank the first one standing in the kitchen, just to prime the pipes. Then he poured a double and sauntered to his chair in the living room, promising himself that was when the sipping would begin.

He was on his third drink, and had yet to sip once.

The television was on but muted. He'd flipped past a talk show, a hockey game, and a sitcom before landing on an old Mel Brooks movie in black and white. He stared at the screen, but barely registered what was happening. The dancing Frankenstein monster made him chuckle, though.

"How did we go from bitching about a guy to planning to kill him?" he muttered. But he didn't really mean it. He knew he *should* be feeling something about the situation, probably guilt or revulsion, but the only emotions he could muster were fear and disappointment.

Fear of getting caught.

Disappointment that Barry was one who got to do the deed, and not him.

It should be him.

"It should be me," Marty said, liking the sound the words made aloud.

Sure, Carson lost out on money because of Tanner, but so what? Tanner didn't take anything out of Carson's pocket. He paid him for his company shares, fair and square. As usual, Carson the inveterate gambler needed the money at the time, so he took it. Sure, he would have had about forty times more if he'd held onto them until Santo Corp bought the company, but that wasn't a real loss. It was a *potential* loss. It was like some guy lamenting that if he'd only bet on the hundred-to-one horse at the Kentucky Derby, he'd have made a bundle.

"Yeah, but you didn't bet," Marty told the imaginary complainer. "And you didn't lose anything, you just didn't win."

He thought about it some more and decided that analogy wasn't perfect, because Carson *did* see some money. The Derby crybaby gambler didn't even get that.

Wanting to kill someone over money? Marty didn't get it. When Santo Corp bought out Chismo, their accounting team took over for the new subsidiary. That meant all of the accounting work he had been doing on contract for Chismo went bye-bye. It wasn't millions, but it was still money. Income that he *actually* lost, unlike Carson's potential loss. But you didn't see him crying over it. There were things far more important than money.

Which brought him to Barry, whose beef he somewhat understood. Tanner's miserly approach to the server upgrade got him hurt, and now his life was forever changed. Fine, Barry had a right to be pissed. He had a point.

But couldn't he just sue the guy? His case was strong, almost airtight. Any lawyer worth a damn would see that, and take him on for a contingency fee. Barry could sting Tanner for a huge load of dough and get on with his life. But instead, he stayed on at Chismo in a diminished role.

That part, he didn't get.

And what was Serena's deal? Why was she so mysterious about her reasons? It couldn't be a trust issue—the four of them were trusting each other with their very freedom by conspiring together. But she kept her cards close, that one.

"She's gotta have a good reason," Marty murmured, and took a sip of his drink.

Ha! A sip!

He was sure he looked elegant doing it, too. His La-Z-Boy wasn't too fancy, but maybe the cigar magazine appreciated the rugged look of an ordinary average guy.

Oh, man.

He was so drunk.

"It should be me," he said firmly, and jabbed his finger toward Gene Wilder on the TV. "He stole my *wife*!" He swirled his glass, looking down into the brown liquid. "My life," he added.

He reached for his phone. He still had pictures of her. Not many, because they weren't the picture-taking kind of couple, but there were a few. He swiped through them rapidly, then returned to the beginning and went through them again. She was smiling in the first two or three. Beautiful, genuine smiles. That's who Andrea was. Or who he thought she was, at least.

As he thumbed through the pictures, though, he noticed that the bloom came off those smiles. Oh, the gesture was still there. Lips curled at the corners, sometimes even teeth shining. But the luster faded. The smiles looked more perfunctory in the later photos, and in some, you could argue she wasn't smiling at all. Maybe that was why he stopped taking photos of her, and they of each other.

Marty cleared his throat as he stared down at the last photograph he had of Andrea. She was in a burgundy blouse, and wore her hair back in a ponytail. He'd surprised her with the shot, and while her expression was natural, it wasn't necessarily a happy one.

She looked like that a lot toward the end, he realized. He'd known it then, but he never thought to ask about it, or to act on it. He just assumed it was a down cycle, something all marriages reportedly went through at times. The key was to outlast it, and wait for the market correction.

But Tanner Fritz was the goddamn market correction. More than a market correction, he was Black-fucking-Monday, a stock market crash.

Marty stared down at the shot of Andrea. He decided to make that image her contact picture on his phone. A few swipes and taps later, he'd saved that curious expression as the one that would pop up when she called.

If she called.

She had no reason to speak to him these days. Nothing connected the two of them anymore. For all he knew, she'd changed her phone number.

Had she?

Before he could think about it further, Marty pressed the green phone button on the screen. Then he pressed the receiver to his ear.

The phone rang three times. He almost hung up after the second ring, but decided to let it go. If he'd taken more decisive action in their marriage instead of spending his time watching *Battlestar Galactica*, maybe Tanner wouldn't have been able to steal her in the first place.

On the fifth ring, the phone clicked. There was a short silence, then he heard Andrea's voice.

"Marty?"

He cleared his throat. "Uh, yeah, hey, An. It's me."

Another silence. It went on so long, he thought she'd hung up.

"An?"

"What do you want, Marty?" Her tone wasn't friendly, but he thought he heard some trace of affection there. Or maybe it was just caution. "What time is it?"

"Kinda late," he admitted. "Sorry. Were you asleep?"

"No. I was reading in bed, but I was thinking about going to sleep. Marty, why are you calling me?"

"Is he there?"

"He? You mean my husband?"

"Yeah, him."

"No. He's out with clients."

"This late?"

She made a slight, almost inaudible sigh before answering. He knew it well. He used to call it her ninja sigh. He could always hear it, that trace of a hidden sigh, and he knew that it meant she was vexed, but there was no chance of ever convincing her she'd made the sound.

"Marty . . ."

"Why are you sighing?"

"I'm not sighing."

"You just did. Right before you said my name."

"Marty . . ." She ninja-sighed again. "You're calling me at an inappropriate hour and asking me if my husband's home. If I were to sigh—and I didn't—but if I did, most of the civilized world would agree that it was warranted. Now what do you want?"

Now Marty sighed, but his was an honest one at least. "I just wanted to talk. To know how you're doing."

"I'm good." She paused for a moment, then asked, "Are you?"

She sounded good. Like how he remembered her right after college, early in their relationship. She didn't sound tired, like she had toward the end of their marriage. For most of it, if he was being honest. Always tired.

Not, not tired. Weary.

She'd sounded weary.

Not tonight, though. Tonight, she sounded good. And sleepy.

"Marty?"

He brushed his hand across his eyes, surprised to find tears spilling out of them. "I'm good, too," he croaked, and reached for his drink. He took a gulp, finishing half of what remained in the glass.

"You sound . . . weird. Or drunk."

"I'm just tired."

She didn't answer. He could imagine the skeptical expression on her face. It was an expression that said, "You're bullshitting me, pal, and not only is that an insult, but it is also a waste of my time. So how about we just skip right to what you really need to say, huh?"

Her expressions tended to be verbose.

She'd fired that exact expression at him fairly frequently throughout their marriage. Sometimes it was even warranted. Now it seemed to be zipping its way sonically to him through the airwaves.

"Okay," he said, trying to ward off the sound of her look. "If I'm being honest, I came across a picture of you on my phone, and so I called you. That's all."

She didn't answer. A spark of hope flickered in his chest.

Seize the day.

"Actually, that's not all," he said. "I called because I still love you, Andrea."

"Marty . . ."

"I want you back."

There, he'd said it.

He forged ahead. "I've changed. Things will be different. *We'll* be different."

"Marty," she said again. He could hear the girl-letting-a-guy-know-she-doesn't-feel-that-way tone creeping into her voice, along with a sadness kicker. Somehow that was worse than the earlier expression he'd imagined, worse than her not sounding weary anymore while sleeping in Tanner Fritz's bed.

"That's not going to happen." She spoke deliberately. "I'm not coming back to you. I... I don't love you. And I'm happy now."

"Okay," he said, sadly accepting his fate. What else could he say?

He waited for her to say she was sorry about it, but when she didn't respond, he pulled the phone away from his ear and jabbed the red icon, ending the call.

Marty clenched and unclenched his jaw. Hurt and anger swirled in his chest, mixing into a poisonous concoction that he couldn't exactly identify. The mix of emotions didn't feel good, but they were resolute.

He looked down at his drink again. "Sipping is for pussies, Tanner," he said, and threw back the remains of his drink.

Chapter Thirteen

Barry

"Honey, maybe you got to go to work?"

Barry stirred, his eyelids lifting slowly to meet the light of day. The first thing he realized was that he was lying in a bed that felt like a cloud. It wasn't his bed. It was her's. He hadn't slept in any bed but his own in years. He looked up at Lena as images of the previous night sprang to mind. She had accosted him as soon as he walked through the door, kissing him, stroking him, and pulling off his clothes. He was immediately rock hard.

"Last night was really something," he said as he caressed her thigh. "You were…"

"Stop the play-by-play, would you? You want the bottom line?"

He nodded.

"I don't trust a man I ain't humped. You were more than adequate, and it looks like I banged the stutter right out of you. Why, listen to yourself, you're so articulate you could MC Late Night with Jimmy Fallon."

He thought about it for a moment. "What?"

"Exactly. You said, *What* not *W-w-what*. I'd say that's the best work I ever did but it wouldn't be true. I once banged the limp out of a guy who had polio since he was six years of age."

"You're kidding, right?"

"No, Barry, I-I'm fucking not. It's a gift—I've got a one-in-a-million spiritual-healing pussy."

He cracked an indulgent smile.

"Oh yeah? Don't believe me, wise guy? Let's to go again. I'll have your hemorrhoids turn around and crawl right back where they came from."

"I'm game." As he reached for her to pull her down on top of him he realized she was right. "I'm game," he repeated as a broad grin rose. "I'm fucking game."

"So that's a *no* as far as going into work I imagine."

"Fuck work. It makes me stutter."

With a pleased smile on her face, she mounted him and took off like the banker thoroughbred at the Kentucky Derby. They crossed the ten-furlong finish line and kept on going.

They screwed and napped. Barry didn't wake up until after eleven. He texted his manager and apologized for the no-show saying he had been up all night with a cough, had fallen asleep just before dawn, and didn't hear the alarm go off. He peed and walked into the kitchen.

Lena wore a calico apron over a pair of white cotton panties. "I'm whipping up breakfast," she said. "You hungry?"

"Just as long as it's not fucking meatloaf." He walked toward her with purpose, picked her up, and slammed her down on the table.

In between moaning and panting, she cried out, "Turn off the goddamn gas. I can't afford to burn down another rental."

Afterward, Lena dried the table and they ate cold eggs and overcooked bacon. The coffee was bitter and he cut it with lots of milk. "It's your fault the breakfast is shit," she said.

"Best meal I ever ate," he said as a strip of brittle bacon crumbled between his fingers. "How are you feeling?"

"Sore but nothing a pint of aloe won't fix. On the plus side, I think that new IUD is now sitting exactly where it belongs." She winked at him. "That accident you were in didn't hurt your long game none. Good thing, too—I can't take no more disappointment in my life. Three deadbeat husbands, no money, and a waitress job that makes my feet ache."

"Three divorces?"

"Nah, widowed."

"Three times?"

"Extenuating circumstances."

Barry was now fully alert. "Extenuating circumstances? Like what?"

Lena sipped her coffee. She didn't seem to care that it was bitter enough to kill off a plague of locusts. "Randolph, he was my first. Dumb son of a bitch went catfish noodling, stuck his hand in a catfish hole, and got bit by a cottonmouth."

Barry cringed. "That's terrible. I'm so sorry."

Lena shrugged. "You get used to it."

"What happened to the other two?"

She put down her mug and looked him squarely

in the eye. "Wood chipper got husband number two. Idiot wore oversized thermals. They got twisted up with some branches he was feeding in and… well, that fucked up about ten yards of mulch."

Barry felt his temples throbbing and began to rub the sides of his head in a circular motion. "My God."

"Want to hear about the last one?"

"Yeah, why not? I'm numb already."

"Blew himself up with a hunting rifle."

Barry gasped. "Blew himself up with a hunting rifle? How does that even happen?"

"Sabotaged ammo."

"S-s-sabotaged ammo?"

"Easy now, my friend. I'm too worn out to fuck the stuttering out of you again. Take a deep breath."

"W-why was there-there sabotaged ammo in his rifle?"

"Simple. I caught him fucking our neighbor's high school daughter."

"Y-you mean-mean you, you?"

"That's right, handsome. Lots of ways of killing a man."

Barry's head dropped. With his hand pressed against his chest he made a conscious effort to slow his breathing and his rampant heart. Lena stood and began stroking his hair.

"Deep breaths, hon. It'll pass. Just give it a minute."

It took several minutes for Barry to regain his composure. When he finally had a grip he looked up into her eyes. "I think," he began, "I think there's a reason we met."

Chapter Fourteen

Carson

"I thought we were going to meet alone, Serena," Carson groused.

She sat across from him, sitting rigidly in the easy chair of Carson's living room. He didn't mind that part. Marty seated next to him is the part he minded.

Serena gave him a disdainful look. "A girl can only take so much self-absorbed dick in one week."

"Dick?" Marty repeated.

"Self-absorbed?" Carson asked.

"Yes," Serena said evenly.

"Yes what?" Carson asked.

"Yes, you are self-absorbed and even in an occasional fuck buddy, it can get old." She turned to Marty. "And yes, Marty, even though it's none of your business, Carson and I still take a lap for old times' sake once in a while."

Marty frowned.

Carson punched him in the arm, not lightly. "Get over it, dude."

Marty rubbed his arm and scowled at Carson. "Get over what?"

"Your little crush on Serena."

"I don't have—"

"She's never going to fuck you. Grow up."

"Grow up?" Marty's eyes widened. "Me? Look who's talking."

"Boys." Serena's spoke softly but the single word stopped them. When she had their attention, she said, "We have a problem. It's Barry."

"I could have told you that from the very beginning," Carson said. Whatever happened to Barry hadn't just changed his friend on the outside. As far as Carson was concerned, the blow to the head had rewired the man's entire way of thinking. "He's a mess, and he never should have been part of this, much less the one who gets to—"

"He won fair and square," Marty interrupted. "Don't be a sore loser about it."

"I'm not being a sore loser. I'm—"

Serena held up her hand, stopping them both again. "Enough. This isn't about Barry winning the draw. It's about how he's going about doing the job."

"Fucking it up, you mean?" Carson was pretty sure whatever plan Barry made would fail. In fact, he was betting on it.

"In a way. He's brought in an accomplice."

Both men stared at her. Finally, Marty sputtered, "An accomplice? I don't understand."

"She's a waitress at a diner he's been going to. But last night, they went back at her place. I'm guessing she served him more than meatloaf."

Carson grinned in spite of himself. "You mean Barry served *her* the meatloaf? Good for him." He looked over at Marty. "Waitresses are awesome."

Marty shook his head in disgust.

"What?" Carson said. "I can't be happy for the

guy? It's not like he gets laid constantly. His sex life is almost as bad as yours, Stitch."

"Nevermind about my love life."

"I didn't say love. That's a whole other disaster. I'm just talking about you getting your weasel greased once in a while."

Marty pointed a finger at his face. "Shut up. You just . . . you shut up."

"Nice comeback, Potsie." He turned to Serena. "Why should we care that the stutterer is getting a little babaganoush in his life?"

"Babaganoush?" Serena repeated, her tone reproving. "Really?"

Carson shrugged. "Seriously, what do I care?"

"You should care. If he brings in a partner, that's one more person who knows about all of this."

"Not if he doesn't tell her."

Serena gave him a knowing glance. "He just got laid for the first time in years. You think he's in a secret-keeping mood right about now?"

"Oh, shit," Carson muttered. She was right. Barry was probably wound so tight that his head nearly exploded when he finally bedded the waitress.

"Oh, shit is right," Serena said. "Now, I did some digging into this woman's background, and—"

"Digging?" Marty gave her a curious look. "Like a private detective? When did you learn to do that?"

"It's called Google," Serena said dismissively. "Now, listen. She's been married three times, and all of her husbands have died."

"That sounds unlucky."

"I don't think it's luck. I think she's a black widow."

An image of a femme fatale sprang up in Carson's mind. He raised an eyebrow. "So she's hot, then?"

"She just fucked Barry. What do you think?"

"Oh." He pushed the image away and tried to concentrate on what Serena was saying. "So if that's true, then she should be good at this."

"One would assume. Which, like I said, would mean that there's a chance—"

"A chance that Barry could actually pull it off," Carson said. He shook his head mournfully. That was *not* the outcome he was betting on. Tanner Fritz was going to die, but *he* was going to do the honors.

"No, moron. I'm not talking about success here. I'm talking about failure, and us ending up in a jam as a result. If they get caught, what's to stop her from selling us out? Or him singing, for that matter?"

"Barry wouldn't do that," Marty asserted.

"*You* wouldn't do that," Serena countered.

"Neither would I," Carson made sure to say. He had to defend his good name, after all.

Serena ignored him, keeping her eyes on Marty. "*You* wouldn't," she repeated. "And under normal circumstances, I'd agree with you about Barry. But if he decides he's in love, all bets are off."

"Maybe they're just fuck buddies," Carson suggested.

She shook her head. "That's not how he was looking at her."

"Jesus," Marty said. "How long did you watch them?"

"Long enough to see it was more than lust."

"That's a little creepy. And why were you following them in the first place?"

"Screw you," Serena said. "I'm the only one looking out for us here. You should be thanking me."

"If Marty was going to thank you for anything, it'd be the striptease from the other day," Carson said. "That had to be a huge deposit in his spank bank."

Marty flushed. "Will you grow up?"

"I am. I get laid. That's how you know I'm a grown up."

"If Barry's girlfriend messes things up, you're both going to prison," Serena said sternly. "The grownups in there are just waiting to get laid, but I don't think either of you will like it."

"Stitch might."

"Screw you, Carson."

Carson shrugged. "Hey, when you're not getting any, at a certain point, sex is sex, right?"

"Then go fuck yourself." Marty turned back to Serena. "What are we going to do?"

She let the question hang in the air. The silence filled with tension as they both waited to hear her answer. Only when she seemed satisfied that she had their full attention did she speak.

"Stop them," Serena said. "We have to stop them."

"How?" Carson asked.

"I have a plan. Left to his own devices, Barry might have tried something quiet, but nothing about this woman or how her husbands died is subtle. She's a bull in a ceramics shop."

"And that's helpful because…?" Marty looked at her expectantly.

"Because I will be keeping an eye on them. When they make their move, I'll make mine. Not only will I thwart Barry's efforts, but I'll make Tanner nervous in the process."

"Nervous people are suspicious," Marty warned.

"Maybe," she agreed. "But they make mistakes, too." Serena gave them both an imperious gaze. "I've got this for now, boys. But stay by your phones in case I need your help."

Chapter Fifteen

Barry

The structure behind the hovel Lena rented was technically a garage in that it housed a vehicle but at a glance the names shack and lean-to might quicker spring to mind. Barry and Lena waited until evening before slipping into the structure. A solitary light bulb hung from the ceiling. Lena flashed a searchlight beam on it and Barry clicked it on by pulling on a string. The sound of fluttering wings immediately made his heart to jump.

"Hit the deck," she yelled as she dove for the floor. Barry dropped on top of her knocking the wind out of her just as a small colony of bats took off through the open door, skyward.

"M-m-m-motherfucker," he swore. "What the hell-hell was that?"

She was still trying to draw breath as she rolled him off. "Oof. Y'almost punctured a damn lungs."

"You said to…"

"And you sure did. What's the matter, never saw a few measly bats before?"

"N-n-n- no." He stood and helped her to her feet.

"Lived your entire life in the city?"

"Yes."

"Well, they're nothing more than flying mice.

What's the big goddamn deal?"

"You're the wuh-one who said, 'Hit the deck,' not me."

"Because I didn't want the stupid pests getting tangled up in my long hair. You've got nothing for them to get trapped in. Anyway, looky here." She strode a few feet to a covered vehicle and whipped a guano-covered tarp off a rusted stake bed truck. The vehicle had started life cherry red but rust had eaten away most of the paint.

"W-what's this?" Barry asked.

"Ain't she pretty? Forty-eight Ford Stakeback."

"Does it r-r-run?"

"Course it does. Runs like a top. How the hell we supposed to execute our plan with a vehicle that doesn't run? Drove here from Hot Springs with it. Didn't give me a lick of trouble."

Barry walked around the vehicle, giving it a once over. A couple of the stake rails were splintered and the windows were covered with so much grime no one would be able to see in. *That's good*, he thought. "Do we have to take off the license plate?"

"No." She spit on the ground. "We'll call more attention to ourselves without one. Besides, that's just some old plate I kyped from a junkyard. It ain't been registered in over ten years."

That was good too. He felt pleased with himself for having taken her into his confidence. Having an ally felt comfortable, and any concern about her was wiped out by the fact that he had something on her—she'd admitted to killing at least one of her husbands. He wasn't worried about her ratting him out if they got caught.

She picked up an old rag and cleared some of the grime from the front windshield, an area just big enough for them to see out. "We'd better get going if we want to be in place when your boss and his rickshaw ho leave the tavern they've been frequenting."

Barry nodded, adrenaline already coursing through him.

Tanner's going to get his.

The driver's door opened with a terrifying creak but she turned the key and the old engine sputtered to life. "Get in," she hollered over the noise of the backfiring exhaust. "We'd better fill the tank before we head on over."

Barry wrestled open the sticking passenger door and climbed aboard. She forced the shifter into first gear and let up on the clutch. The old truck sputtered and lurched forward with a loud fart from the exhaust but kept on going out the driveway and into the night.

Lena produced a pair of knit hats that they both donned along the way. Barry was impressed.

She's thought of everything.

There was a dark alleyway just down the block from Tanner's hideaway. Lena backed the old truck into it as far as she could without compromising their view of the pub's doorway.

"So now we just wait?" Barry asked.

"What would you like us to do, light a bag of shit on fire and hope he comes out to step on it?" She pointed at the Lamborghini. "The yellow dickmobile is parked outside. That means your boy is inside with the Chinese eggplant. Waiting is all we can do. You sure you want to go through with this?"

"Yes, I hate him. I want him to d-die."

"You're sure?"

"Yes."

"Because a few more sessions with my therapeutic coochie and you'll be right as rain. I told you what it did for that polio boy. He became a track and field star."

"It doesn't change anything. I t-told him over and over again that he-he needed to hire professionals but he didn't listen. He was more interested in the b-bottom line."

"All right, then. No skin off my nose. Let's waste this loser."

More than thirty-minutes passed before Barry saw the restaurant door open and a woman with long tanned legs step out into the night. "That's her," Barry said startling his dozing accomplice. "H-hurry, switch places."

"Huh?"

"I have to do it. It has to be me," Barry said. "Hurry."

"All right," Lena said as she leapfrogged over him onto the passenger seat. "Sure you can handle it?"

"I'm sure." He turned the key and the seventy-year old engine shook to life. Barry reached for the shifter and tried to push it into gear but it wouldn't go.

"Clutch, clutch!" she yelled. "You've got to press down on the clutch."

"What?"

"Haven't you ever driven a manual?"

"A what?"

"A manual shift."

"N-no."

"Shit. Move your leg. I'll get it into gear for you then you hit the gas. Got it?" He nodded and she squeezed her leg in between his. "Give it gas," she said as she shifted and eased up on the clutch. Barry accelerated and she jumped backward into her seat. The truck rambled forward just as Tanner came out of the restaurant and stepped to his date's side. They walked up the block together in the direction of the yellow sports car.

"There they are," Lena said. "Hang back until they begin to cross the street. Then floor it and knock that sack of shit into tomorrow."

He followed her instructions to the letter, allowing the truck to roll so slowly its forward motion was barely perceptible. Up ahead, Tanner stepped into the street.

"Now!" she hollered. "Mash it!"

Barry slammed on the gas as Tanner reached the middle the street. The truck shot forward. Out the corner of his eye he saw a small boy of ten of twelve running toward Tanner with a legal-sized manila envelope in his hand. The truck was headed right at the kid. Barry tried to turn the wheel but the old truck didn't have power steering and the wheel was rigid. He used all his might to veer off, missing the mystery boy and Tanner, but he had overcompensated. The truck bounced up onto the sidewalk. Tanner's leggy companion screamed as the truck slammed into a fire hydrant. The thrust of the released water propelled the hydrant yards into the air. Water exploded from the large chasm in the street, hitting the woman squarely in the torso, rocketing her upward, and dropping her flat on her face.

The old truck sped off, but in the wind Barry could hear the Asian woman screaming at the top of her lungs. He glanced in the side mirror to see her hopping around, clutching her chest. To his dismay, a perfectly safe Tanner Fritz ran to her assistance while a confused kid stood holding out the envelope.

Barry took the corner and drove like hell.

Chapter Sixteen

Carson

Carson looked around Barry's living room. "Dude, your place sucks."

Barry didn't react. He was staring down at his hands.

"Seriously, who's your interior designer? An ex-prison warden?" When Barry didn't respond, Carson sighed and sank onto the gray couch next to Serena. She pointedly shifted away from him, scowling.

What's her problem? There'd always been an ebb and flow to their casual sexual relationship, and when it ebbed, her mild irritation with him turned into outright disdain. He was used to it even though it disheartened him, but this recent behavior seemed like something more.

He wondered for a second if she'd met someone. That would explain her shift in behavior. He decided the odds were good that was the reason. She'd met someone and was coming to grips with the fact that it probably meant the days of their occasional dalliances were over.

I'll have to let her know I'm still DTF, even if she's with someone else. Even and occasional friend with benefits—no complaints, not with an ass like hers.

He didn't care if it was technically cheating. For one thing, it was cheating for her, not for him. And for another, Serena was a wildcat he never got tired of screwing. So, if maintaining some semblance of their arrangement required a little bit of sneaking around? Well, he was down for that, as well.

"What are you smiling about?" Marty demanded.

"I'm smiling?"

"Like an idiot."

"Sure you're not looking in a mirror?"

"I'm not that ugly."

Carson smiled bigger. His relationship with Marty had ebb and flow, too. Marty vacillated from complete omega wolf to deciding to show his teeth and bark a little. All it usually took to put him back in his place was a smackdown on the racquetball court or some other physical drubbing. The prospect of that always made Carson smile.

"I'm a happy guy," he explained.

"No money problems, huh?"

Carson scowled. "Mind your business."

Low blow, asshole.

"Will you two shut *the fuck* up?" Serena snapped. She looked over at Barry. "Why are we here, Barry? Do you have a plan?"

Barry glanced up sharply, then looked away. "N-no. No plan."

Carson threw up his hands. "Then what? You're throwing in the towel? Or maybe you want us to come up with a plan for you? Well, forget it. You drew the straw, you make the plan."

Barry shook his head. "I-I don't n-need your stupid plan, C-Carson."

"My plan is brilliant." *To let yours fail so it becomes my turn.*

"You have a plan?" Marty asked. "Why do you have a plan?"

Carson gave him a knowing look. What was Marty's problem? They already had this conversation, and he knew what Carson meant. Was he trying to out him to the others?

"I meant," Carson explained, "that *if* I had to come up with a plan, it would be awesome."

"You'd probably try to bash his head in with a racquet and pretend it was an equipment malfunction," Marty said. "Or push him out into traffic."

Barry moaned.

"And what would you do?" Carson sneered. "Find a way to screw up his tax return so he goes to prison and gets shanked in the shower?"

"That's actually not a bad plan," Marty said.

"It's horrible. Who do you know in prison? How's the shanking gonna happen?"

"I don't need to set it up," Marty said. "A guy like Tanner Fritz would get himself shanked inside of a week if he went to prison."

Carson scoffed. "The way he can bullshit people? By the end of the first week, he'd have the parole board setting him free and the other prisoners voting him most likely to succeed."

Marty opened his mouth to reply, then closed it. "Tanner-goddamn-Fritz," he muttered.

"Tanner-goddamn-Fritz," Carson agreed. "

Barry moaned again.

The three of them turned to him. Barry looked

miserable.

"Barry?" Serena asked, her tone reassuring.

Barry refused to meet anyone's gaze. "I tried," he said. "I tried to do it, but it d-didn't work."

They fell silent.

Je-sus, Carson thought. *Is he saying what I think he is?*

Finally, Marty spoke up. "You already tried to do... *it?*"

Barry nodded.

"Holy *shit*," Carson muttered.

This was great. When Serena said they'd need to stop Barry and his girlfriend, he had no idea how they'd manage to do it. Now, it seemed like he didn't have to worry about it after all.

"What happened?" Serena asked.

Barry swallowed hard. "I-I tried to r-run him over when he was crossing the street. Outside a c-club."

"In your *own car?*" Serena asked.

Barry looked confused. "N-no," he stammered. "I borrowed it."

"From who?"

Barry shifted uncomfortably. "A f-friend."

"What friend?"

He looked up and gave her a defiant stare. "It doesn't matter. Some kid got in the way, so I had sw-swerve to miss them all. I hit a f-fire hydrant instead."

The three paused, taking in the information. Then Carson laughed. "You murdered a fire hydrant, Barry? That's classic. I bet water went everywhere."

"It did. Knocked over Tanner's date."

Marty sat up straight. "Wait. He had a date?"

Barry nodded. "I think her tits exploded."

Carson laughed harder.

Marty stared at Barry in disbelief. "His date?"

Barry nodded.

"As in girlfriend?"

"I guess."

"Whose car was it, Barry?" Serena asked. Her voice held a low menace.

"Nobody's," Barry said. "It doesn't matter. I drove away."

"What if someone saw the car? Or got the license plate?"

"The plate is s-stolen." Barry's stutter re-emerged again. "The ve-vehicle is unr-r-registered. It's fine."

Serena glared at him. Barry squirmed but said nothing further.

Carson clapped his hands together. "So that's that. Barry tanked. My turn."

"Why is it your turn?" Marty objected.

"Because I'm next."

"Says who?"

Carson gave Marty a warning look. "*I* do."

Marty was undeterred. "We should draw straws again. That's the only fair way."

"Where's the car, Barry?" Serena asked, ignoring Carson and Marty.

This irritated Carson. Why was she harping on this? "Hey, let it go," he said. "Let's move on to my plan."

Serena threw up her hands. "Fucking amateurs," she snapped. She stood without another word, stormed to the front door of Barry's small apartment, opened it and left, slamming the door behind her.

"What's her problem?" Carson asked.

"She doesn't want us to get caught," Marty said.

"Then why let the dummy here go first?" Carson asked.

"I'm not d-d-dumb!" Barry yelled forcefully. "I have a b-b-brain injury, you fuckhead!"

"Yeah, Carson," Marty added. "You fuckhead."

Carson raised his hands, placating. "Okay, okay. Sorry, buddy. I shouldn't have said that. But you did blow it, right?"

Barry trembled with fury as he glared at Carson, but after a few moments, he dropped his gaze. "Yeah," he muttered.

"Then it's my turn," Carson proclaimed.

"No," Marty said, his tone hard. "We draw straws."

"Marty—"

"He's right," Barry grunted. He pulled a handful of coins from his pocket and fished out a quarter. "Only t-two of you, so we'll flip."

Carson frowned, but he couldn't see any way around it short of threatening physical force, and while that might work in small doses with Marty, it ran the risk of ruining the friendship if overdone. Carson had drinking buddies and gambling buddies, but Marty had been right about one thing—he had no real friends outside of these two. So he acquiesced. "But I call it," he insisted.

Marty shrugged. "Fine."

Barry hesitated, then used his thumb to send the coin spinning in the air. Carson watched it, waiting for his muse to push him the right way. It was a sixth sense he had, one that made him a skilled gambler. He'd learned to trust it over the years.

As the coin descended into Barry's waiting palm, Carson called out, "Heads."

Barry turned the coin over, slapping it onto his forearm. Both Carson and Marty leaned forward to see the silver image of the spread-winged eagle.

"Ha!" Marty whooped.

"Shit," Carson said.

Carson sighed. *Barry must have cheated somehow.* He eyed him suspiciously, but Barry's expression was guileless. Still, there was no way his muse had been wrong.

"Ha!" Marty repeated.

"Oh, shut up, Marty," Carson said. He stood up and headed toward the door. "Have at it, then. I'm sure you'll fuck it up at least as bad as Barry did."

Marty said something as he left, but Carson cut off his comeback midway through as he closed the door behind himself. He stomped down the stairs, feeling the frustration in his chest. *Barry cheated, and once again, the whole process wasn't fair.* He hoped he might at least catch up to Serena and try to angle for a pity fuck. Or at least some pity head. He bet he could talk her into it.

But Serena was nowhere in sight.

Chapter Seventeen

Marty

He took his time driving home. The glow of having beaten Carson at something, *anything*, was something he wanted to revel in. Sure, it was a goddamn coin flip, but still. He beat Carson, the macho jock, alpha male, high-speed cocksman, and even better, with Barry as a witness.

Marty imagined the fallout. From here on out, whenever he got into an argument with Carson, he could just pull out a quarter and start flipping it in the air, saying nothing. Seeing the silver coin spinning in the air would flummox the normally unflappable Carson, and Marty would win the argument.

"Suck it, Carson," he shouted to his empty car.

He stopped for a red light. As much as it felt good to gloat, it didn't take long for him to start feeling a little bad for Carson. Sure, his friend put up a huge bravado front, but he knew things weren't going his way, and hadn't been since the Chismo buyout. Maybe earlier, but definitely since. His gambling problem seemed to get steadily worse. Marty knew he'd been demoted from sales manager to salesman at work, even though he tried to claim the move was one he chose for the opportunity to make more money. And there was no way to color the bankruptcy that Marty had guided him through as anything other than what it was—financial disaster.

Carson may be an asshole, but he's my friend.

Still, beating him once in a while felt good.

Marty turned his mind to the problem at hand. If he was going to do a better job of killing Tanner Fritz than Barry, he'd need a better plan than trying to run the man down in a car.

A variety of ideas flitted through his mind, but all of them involved too much direct action. He shared Serena's caution about getting caught. What good would it do to succeed in getting revenge on Tanner if he ended up in prison for his troubles? Or on Death Row?

The car behind him honked, and Marty continued driving home. He racked his mind about everything he knew about Tanner. Nothing immediately jumped out at him as a possibility, and thinking about Tanner only succeeded in taking some of the wind out of his sails, deflating his earlier satisfaction at beating Carson.

The problem was that on the surface, Tanner seemed like a great guy to many people. He kept up an image that people liked. Hell, at one time, that was probably who he truly was. In college, Tanner was the one who made sure everyone was included. He always made Marty feel like he was his best friend. And even though he knew it wasn't exactly true, since everyone else in their group was also his best friend, it still felt good. That started changing once college ended and Tanner and Carson started up Chismo. They drifted apart, and Tanner became whoever he was now. An image, a façade that few took the time to look deep enough to see the real man beneath—the kind of guy who would steal a man's wife, for instance.

So he searched through his memory for any weaknesses, any failings he could exploit. The information about Tanner having a girlfriend on the side might be useful if his goal was to break up Tanner's marriage and win Andrea back. He didn't see how it could help him with killing the man, though. Telling Andrea might break her heart but it wouldn't drive her to murder.

By the time he made it home, he could only think of two faults. Tanner didn't know how to ski, and he was allergic to peanut butter.

"How can I use that?" Marty grumbled, flopping onto his couch.

Maybe he could get Tanner up on the slopes and then push him down one of the high difficulty courses. But Marty could barely ski himself, so how was that supposed to work? Besides, knowing Tanner, the guy would figure out how to ski on the fly, and end up setting a record for fastest time or something.

"I could force-feed him a peanut butter and jelly sandwich," Marty groused. "Minus the jelly."

That was about as good a plan as the ski trip he had envisioned. Making a guy to eat something he's deathly allergic to? Impossible. Especially an athletic man like Tanner. Even Carson wouldn't be able to manage that.

Trying to trick him was another possibility, but that would be a tough go, too. Tanner was careful about his allergy, because it was so acute. He avoided peanut butter like his life depended on it, since it pretty much did.

But what if he camouflaged it? Wrapped it in something he *did* like? Would that work? By the time Tanner knew he'd put the peanut butter in his mouth, it'd be too late, right?

But how?

Then Marty smiled.

"Oh, yes," he murmured. It was so easy once he thought of it through that lens.

"This will work," he said. "It's genius."

Chapter Eighteen

Barry

"It's about fucking time," Lena growled, bursting out of the bathroom the moment Marty left. "I diddled myself twice waiting for all the BS to subside."

"Y-you what?"

"You heard me, I diddled myself... *twice*. What the hell was I supposed to do to kill all that time? Good thing no one had to come in and take a squirt. They would've been in for one hell of a surprise."

"You-you're kind of worked up. Maybe you should..."

"Of course I am—with a bunch of whiny-ass children, bitching and moaning about *it's my turn, no, my turn* and such, all the while verbally whooping your butt to boot. I wanted to come out and kick some ass. No one talks to my man like that. Which one of those two doofuses called you a dummy?"

"That was C-Carson."

"Why do you take guff from him? He got me so mad I wanted to knock his teeth out but like I said, I was in mid-diddle."

"He apologized."

"Apologized, a horse's patoot. You can't let a

bully get away with shit like that. Once they see they can get away with it they'll never stop. Did he talk to you like that before you got hurt?"

"N-not so much. Carson was always a d-dick b-but he had more respect for me be-before."

Lena's forehead wrinkled. "And you call this man your friend? He knows who you were—what happened to you. He should be sympathetic, not abusive. I tell you what, after we do Tanner we'll deep six this Carson tool for good measure."

Barry fell into a chair. His face grew pale.

"What's with ya?" she asked. "You look like you just saw a ghost."

"Kill Carson? I-I never…"

"Well, why not? What he's doing is worse than what Tanner done. Sure, it was the accident that fucked you up and Tanner was negligent but he didn't knowingly put you in danger. This Carson on the other hand—he's a real piece of garbage. Calling you names… the fucking nerve of that jerk."

"I don't think I could ever do that. I know he c-c-can be an asshole but we're friends."

"You were friends with Tanner until he got rich. I think all y'all resent him more for his money than for what happened to each of y'all."

"M-m-maybe, but I don't want to kill Carson, and I don't like the idea of killing."

"But you're okay killing Tanner?"

"Yuh-yeah. Because. I'm not a k-killer. I'm just getting even with Tanner."

"Well, if you don't want to get *even* with Carson, let's do the next best thing."

"L-like what?"

"He's so hell bent on being the one who kills Tanner, let's deny him the opportunity."

"What do you mean?"

"Nothing stopping us from going at Tanner again. We can do it right now."

"No. We had our chance."

"Horseshit, we're talking *murder* and you're worrying about playing fair? I say we come up with a better plan and execute it, pronto. All your stupid friends fighting over who got crapped on worse, complaining they're all victims—never heard nothing so stupid."

"You really think we should?"

She sat down next to him on the sofa and stroked his cheek. "Be the man y'are in bed, Barry. Show everyone you're the boss like what you showed me. It's high time you stopped taking everyone's shit." She got on top of him, straddling him, kissing him and pushing his head against the back cushion as she began to grind against him. "Those two diddles did nothing but get me going. You ready to be the boss?"

"Yes," he purred.

She smacked his face. "Think I want to get fucked by a damn wuss? Say it like a man, damn it."

"YES!"

"That's better," she said and unbuckled his belt.

Chapter Nineteen

Serena

Serena lay prone, snugging the rifle butt into the pocket of her shoulder. She centered the sights on the middle of the dark silhouette target down-range, took a shallow breath, and held it. Gently, she squeezed the trigger. The gentle kick of the rifle was just enough to remind her how much power she was wielding.

The power of life and death.

She lined up the target and went through the entire process again. The most difficult part was the trigger pull. Not that it was physically hard to manage, as the actual force required was minimal for the hair trigger. But the range instructor, who had been only too happy to give her private lessons, had been very clear that she should pull slowly and that the actual moment the gunfire erupted to should be a surprise even to her.

That idea was abhorrent to her. Control was her thing. She struggled for a long while to accept this idea of being surprised, and never succeeded. She always knew the exact millisecond the trigger would reach the point of no return and the firing pin would engage.

After her initial guided lesson, she practiced with

her rifle alone. Her solo sessions were oddly satisfying, almost meditative. She experienced a particular thrill when she retrieved her used target to see where her shots had landed. Initially, she was happy just to get a round inside the black silhouette. As she gradually improved, she took great satisfaction in seeing most of her rounds clumped together either at center mass or the head, depending on where she'd focused.

She learned from the instructor what the purpose of the surprise moment was, too. The technique was intended to keep the shooter from jerking the trigger, instead squeezing it gradually. A jerked trigger, he told her, meant a flier round.

He could have just told her that from the beginning, and saved her some time. But Serena was used to enduring how most instruction catered to the lowest common denominator. If she was being honest, she had to do the same thing when she taught the mandatory sexual harassment or cultural sensitivity courses for Chismo.

No. Not for Chismo anymore. For Santo Corp.

Serena lined up another shot. Took a breath and held it. Squeezed.

The gun barked.

Barry and his little tart were going to be a problem, she knew. Left to his own devices, Barry would stand aside after his failed attempt. But this waitress chick? She had a feeling Lena Pretty wasn't going to let thing go so easily.

That situation had to be dealt with.

Marty wasn't going to handle it. He was focusing on whatever eventually bungled attempt he was planning to make on Tanner. The whole thing was amusing, in a dangerous way. She had no doubt Marty would fail, but hoped he would do so quietly. And who knew, maybe the attempt alone would exorcise his demons where Andrea was concerned.

If that eventually happened, maybe she could renew her efforts where he was concerned. She could use a partner on her antiquing trips, but only once Marty was properly molded.

Carson having to wait his turn was something she allowed herself to savor. While she enjoyed the occasional dalliance with him, the guy was a selfish and clumsy lover. Taking his time was not in his repertoire. She could only imagine how much it was driving him crazy to be on the bench while a couple of what he no doubt saw as junior varsity nerds got playing time. She'd made sure it happened the first time, easily rigging the straw drawing event. Carson losing the coin toss was straight up good fortune, allowing Marty to get his chance and Carson to stew about it.

Only, she knew he wasn't going to sit idly by and simmer in his own juices. He'd find a way to sabotage Marty if he could. She was genuinely curious to see if he was able to do so, or if Marty would outsmart him.

She fired again, trying her best to put this bullet through the same hole as the last one.

After Marty failed, Carson would try. She wondered if it might be best if he were successful. Did she really need to be the one to actually drop the hammer on Tanner to get satisfaction from his death? She didn't think so, not if she could be the force behind it happening.

She'd have to wait to see what Carson had in mind when his turn came. And if he happened to blow it, too?

Serena lined up her final shot and sent the round down-range.

If her turn came, she had an answer for that.

Finished, she rose and signaled the range master. No one else was on the range, so he gave her the thumbs up. She trudged the hundred yards to retrieve her target. On the way back, she examined where her bullets had punched holes. There was a clumping near center mass, with a couple of rounds closer to the outside, where the love handles would be on a man. Not perfect, but easily acceptable.

The two rounds she'd fired at the head had landed near the center, looking like a pair of off-kilter eyes that stared back at her for the remainder of the walk back to her shooting position. The crazy eyes made her think of Ms. Lena Pretty.

Serena gathered her rifle and gear and made her way back to the range house, deep in thought. Absently, she flirted with the range master, since she never knew when she might need something from him. A part of her never stopped working the problem over in her mind.

This continued as she drove home, and even after she stowed her rifle and washed her hands. She poured herself a glass of wine and retrieved her leather-bound photo album from the locked cabinet beside the couch.

Flopping back on the cushion, she turned the pages. Part of her enjoyed the trip down memory lane, but another part still whittled away at the Lena Pretty problem.

A plan began to congeal. Initially, she had thought talking to Lena might work, threatening her if necessary, but now she knew that wouldn't cut it. But she had to do something about this woman's influence.

I can't have the waitress in control. No, no no.

She was moving chess pieces in her head while she flipped slowly through her photo book. Move, countermove, then examine the board. Slowly, the pieces were falling into place. She didn't like how close to home all of this had landed, but it was oddly exciting at the same time. She had to mitigate her own risk, though. She had to get a complete handle on the situation before she was arrested along with the three jackasses. *First degree attempted murder, that's a stiff one—life sentence with the possibility of parole—ten years minimum. No way I'm going down for that. I've got to control this stupidity.*

She stared down at the photo book. *But how? That's the question.*

Then it dawned on her. Why hadn't she thought of this before? The answer was right in front of her all along.

Serena sipped her wine and smiled.

Chapter Twenty

Marty

Game face, Marty thought, and rang the doorbell.

When no one answered, he rang again. Another long pause got his heart racing. What if she didn't work from home anymore? What excuse could he possibly manufacture to drop in on her at her place of business? And if he couldn't plant the seeds today, tomorrow night would be a complete nothing. He'd have to rethink his entire approach.

Just as he was debating whether to ring the doorbell again or give up entirely, he heard footsteps. The lock clicked and the door swung open. Belinda Torres gave him a look of surprise. She wore an apron and her luxurious dark hair was up—not how he preferred it but a tuft had escaped her hair clip and now lay across her shoulder. The woman was sexy without trying and since Andrea . . . it didn't take much to bring his blood to a boil.

"Marty? I didn't expect you."

Marty tried to regain the game face he'd lost when it took so long for her to answer the door. "Sorry I didn't call first. I was hoping to catch Carlos."

Not really—just look at those curves.

"Oh, he just left about five minutes ago."

I know. I watched him drive away.

"Dang," Marty said. "I wanted to get his opinion on some new accounting software, to see if he's using it yet. I guess I'll just email him."

"He only went to the store to pick up a few things," Belinda said. "He'll be back soon, if you want to wait."

"That'd be great," Marty said. "Thanks."

Belinda opened the door and let him inside. "Can I get you something? Coffee, tea?"

Me? He added, indulging the fantasy.

"No, I don't want to be any trouble."

"Marty, how could you be trouble?"

"Coffee sounds great. Thanks."

Belinda smiled and headed to the kitchen. Marty followed.

"Did I catch you in the middle of something?" he asked nonchalantly. When she looked at him questioningly, he motioned toward her attire. "The apron?" It tied across the front of her skirt, but didn't cover her sumptuous rear. Marty enjoyed her every step of the way.

"Oh, of course. Yes, I'm getting an order together for a catering event tomorrow night. You can be my guinea pig."

Being called a rodent never excited him so much. The appeal of a curvy backside was never lost on him. Andrea used to move him that way, with the sway of her hips in her skintight yoga pants. He imagined himself pressed against her, believing she'd want him to go further. "Oh, that's right. Your business. Anything fun?"

She removed a cup from the cupboard and filled it from the pot. "I'm sure it'll be fun for the guests, but it's a lot of work for me, and we're only contracted for the appetizers and desserts. Megan Chenowyth got the contract for dinner."

"What's the event?"

"This company is putting on a fundraiser for a children's cancer charity. It's a nice cause, but the place will be packed with corporate types."

"Hey, those corporate types are some of my best clients. Same with Carlos." *Carlos, you lucky son of a bitch.*

She laughed, and set Marty's coffee on the counter next to him. "I suppose so. I wish I had more of them for my business, to be honest."

"I'd be happy to comb my contact list for anyone you might be able to solicit. You could use my name to get in the door."

"That's very generous." She kissed him on the cheek, then rubbed her lipstick away with her thumb. "Carlos is lucky to have a friend like you."

"Your husband's a good guy." He could still feel her lips on his cheek. *Could it be that he's lousy in the sack?* Marty picked up his coffee and took a drink. He wanted to indulge himself further but Carlos was just minutes away. *Better switch gears.* "What company are you catering for?"

"Chismo."

Marty feigned surprise over the rim of his cup. "Really? They're one of my clients. Or they were, before Santo Corp bought them."

"What a funny coincidence," Belinda said. "Small world, I guess."

"It is," he agreed. "But the truth is, I only had the account because I did the work cheap during

No Dibs On Murder

Chismo's startup period."

"Why'd you do that? Carlos won't even give our relatives a family rate on their taxes."

Marty grinned dutifully. "Maybe I should adopt that policy. No, I gave them a discount because I went to college with the founder of Chismo. Tanner Fritz?"

Belinda's expression changed. Marty saw her shift into business mode the moment she heard Tanner's name.

"That's who is giving the keynote address," she said. "And I'm catering the green room."

"Yeah?" Marty worried he was pushing the nonchalant thing. He didn't want to appear dense. Belinda knew better than that. "He's kind of a big deal. One of those guys who other people listen to. If you can impress him..."

She nodded. "It'd be a great reference to have."

"Yeah, people seem to really like him."

Belinda gave him a curious look. "You don't?"

His heart hammered. Was he that transparent?

"No," he said. "I mean, yes. I like him, too. We've grown apart some since college, but you know how those things go."

"Sure," she said. "Outside of family, most of Carlos's friends are work-related, and pretty superficial."

"Same for me," Marty said.

Belinda's eyes widened. "Oh, I'm sorry, Marty. I just realized how that sounded."

"It's okay. It's true. We don't really know each other all that well."

Which is exactly why this will work.

He was grateful he wasn't closer to Carlos and Belinda, and had only gotten to know them after the divorce. If Belinda knew about Andrea marrying Tanner, this whole charade would never have worked.

Marty continued, "I didn't even remember you had a catering business until you said something."

That felt more like an insult than an apology, but somehow it seemed to smooth over the conversational hiccup. The only downside was that a silence then ensued, and as it drew on, it became awkward. Belinda stood near the coffee pot, rocking on her heels. Marty sipped at his coffee. Eventually that gave him an idea.

"Good coffee," he said.

"Thanks."

More silence.

Marty wondered if the realization that she didn't know him very well made her uncomfortable. Like maybe he was a serial killer or something, and she just didn't know it. He had to set her at ease. Convince her that he was harmless. But what could he say?

Maybe *Good thing I'm not a serial killer, huh?*

Or *Look how harmless I am—just harmless Marty the accountant angling to make you an accomplice, and maybe get you out of your panties.*

His best might be simple honesty. *I'd never hurt you, Belinda. I only murder assholes who steal my wife.*

He cleared his throat. "Uh, so what goes into a menu for that sort of event?"

"Oh, the usual," she said, and listed the type of

fare that Marty had seen at every catered event he'd ever been to. Belinda seemed happy to have something neutral to talk about, and she rattled off all of the items with professional pride. He didn't hear anything about her rum balls, though.

"What about dessert?"

"Fruit," Belinda said. "Some chocolates. And my hot buttered rum surprises, of course."

And there it is! Hot buttered Belinda and her rum surprise. Hot diggity!

Marty resisted sighing with relief. "Hot buttered rum?" he repeated, keeping with the nonchalant tone. "If I remember right, Tanner loves hot buttered rum."

"Really?"

"Yeah, he was always mad for it," Marty assured her.

"What about peanut butter? That's the surprise, in the center. Do you know if he likes that?"

Marty smiled. "Who doesn't like surprises?"

Belinda grinned. "That's great. Thanks, Marty."

Marty nodded nonchalantly, as cool as James Bond, he figured. He took another sip of his coffee, which really was good. He hadn't lied about that. Nor had he lied about people liking surprises.

Not Tanner, but people.

Chapter Twenty-One

Carson

Carson angled the shot so that Marty would have to dive for the ball. When the smaller man did so, Carson congratulated himself. Marty slid to his knees, reaching out with his racquet. He surprised Carson by getting the edge of it on the zipping blue ball, but his shot ricocheted straight up. Meanwhile, Marty toppled to the ground, striking his elbow on the floor.

"Ouch!" Marty grimaced and grasped his elbow as the ball bounced next to him, then dribbled into a corner.

"Point!" Carson boomed. "Whooo!"

If this were a beer commercial, he'd hold out his hand to Marty, who would reluctantly take hold as the bigger man heaved him to his feet. They'd share a competitively tinged smile before one of them suggested a rematch—for a beer, of course.

But this was real life, so Carson did what happens in real life.

"Get up, Stitch!" Carson hollered. "Don't be a nancy!"

Marty remained still for a few moments, rubbing his elbow and scowling. Then he slowly clambered to his feet.

"Nice play," he grudgingly conceded.

"Nice? It was *perfect*."

Marty shrugged and went to retrieve the ball.

"Admit it," Carson said, spinning his racquet. "I'm the superior athlete."

"Okay, Ivan Drago," Marty muttered.

"Drago?" Carson shook his head. "No, man. I'm more like the Terminator."

Marty bent over and picked up the rubber ball. "You know he's the bad guy in that movie, right?"

"Says you. He kicks ass."

"Sure. And then he loses. Every time." Marty tossed the ball to Carson, who snatched it out of the air.

"That just proves an important point."

"That movies today are formulaic and derivative?"

Carson's eyes narrowed. Why did Marty always have to try to sound so smart? It was annoying.

"No," he said. "That movies aren't like real life. If those movies really happened, the Terminator would crush everyone and win, and that would be it. Game over, man."

"That's *Aliens*."

"What?"

"Nothing," Marty said.

Carson glowered at him. "Are you being a smart ass?"

"No. I'm just making sure I understand your point."

"What's so hard about it? You make everything more complicated than it needs to be."

Something flashed in Marty's eyes. Carson smiled

slightly. That one must have hit pretty close to home.

"Let me see if I got this," Marty said. He turned toward the wall and dangled his racquet in front of him, prepared for Carson's serve. "You're saying that if an aggressive AI took over all the world's weapons and systematically tried to wipe out mankind, even going to the point of mastering time travel and sending a cybernetic organism back in time to destroy the savior of the human race . . . you're saying that if that *extremely likely* scenario occurred, the machines would win."

Carson bounced the ball once and swung as hard as he could. The blue ball leapt from his racquet and whizzed toward Marty, striking him in the buttocks.

Marty squealed and jumped in the air. "Hey, what the hell?"

"Oops." Carson gave him an 'aw shucks' shrug. "Your point, I guess."

"You did that on purpose!"

"Oh, really? But you weren't being a smart ass?"

Marty dropped his eyes, chagrined slightly. He rubbed his ass cheek with his free hand. "Maybe I was, but you didn't have to resort to physical violence. Besides, your line of thought was ridiculous."

"Ridiculous, huh? Who do you think Tanner is, Stitch? He's the goddamn Terminator."

Marty pursed his lips, considering. "I . . . I don't think the analogy fits."

"Sure it does. The man has . . . what was the word you used? Oh, yeah. He has *systematically* destroyed our lives. And so far, he's unstoppable. Barry tried to run him down with a car, for chrissakes, and that didn't work."

Marty glanced around frantically and shushed him.

Carson waved him away. "No one can hear us in here. It's soundproof."

"No, it's not," Marty said. "It's the exact opposite. So shut up."

Carson cocked his head at Marty. Was he right? Carson had always believed the court was like a cone of silence. If that wasn't true, he shuddered to think of the things people might have overheard during some of the matches he'd played with clients.

"Let's finish the game," Carson said.

Marty shook his head. "I can't."

"Don't be a quitter."

"I can't finish," Marty said. "My knee hurts, my elbow is throbbing, and now my glute feels like it's going to cramp."

"You're going to quit because of an *ass cramp?*"

Marty spun the racquet, loosening the wrist string. Then he took the racquet in his left hand. "I'm done."

"Fine," Carson said. "But that's an injury forfeit."

Marty shrugged. He made his way out of the court. Carson started to follow, then hesitated. He remained inside until Marty shut the door.

"Hey, Stitch," he called out.

Marty stopped and turned to him from the hallway outside the court. He raised his hands questioningly.

"You eat donkey dick," Carson said, keeping his voice at a normal speaking tone.

Marty scowled and fired him a middle finger.

"Huh," Carson grunted.

Marty was right—so much for his soundproof racquetball court theory. It did solve a couple of mysteries regarding lost clients, though.

As they were leaving the gym in Marty's car, Carson spotted Tanner's yellow Lamborghini pulling into the lot. He watched as Tanner lurched into a parking space, barely slowing until the last second. A moment later, Mr. Wonderful popped out of the car and headed toward the front doors of the gym.

"Jesus. I can't get away from this guy."

"None of us can," Marty said. "But that's all going to change soon enough."

Carson tore his eyes away from his nemesis. "I know. So hurry up with blowing your shot so that I can take care of business."

Marty smiled mysteriously. "I don't think you'll get that chance."

"Oh, you've got a plan now?"

"I do. And it's perfect."

"Nothing you've ever done is perfect, Stitch."

A momentary shadow passed over Marty's features, and Carson wondered for a moment if he'd gone too far. Marty had to know he was teasing, right?

"My plan will work," Marty insisted.

Carson decided to try to be supportive. What did it matter? Marty was going to fail either way, so it cost him nothing. "Let's hear it."

"Why should I tell you?"

"You don't want to troubleshoot your plan? That seems a little reckless."

Marty considered, but Carson knew he wouldn't be able to help himself. He'd always craved Carson's approval, and this attempt on Tanner's life was undoubtedly the biggest action he'd ever taken. He'd want Carson to give him the thumbs up on it. He only had to wait it out, and Marty would spill.

It took all of six seconds before Marty asked, "You know how Tanner is allergic to peanut butter?"

"No."

"That figures. I mean, really, Carson...do you know anything about any of us?"

"I know what matters."

"A deadly allergy to peanut butter doesn't matter?"

"It's not like I'm going to stuff peanut butter in his mouth." He stopped and peered at Marty. "Wait a second. Is that your plan?"

"Not exactly. But getting him to eat peanut butter is the end goal, yeah."

"Will it kill him?"

"From what he's always told us, it should."

"Wow." Carson marveled at that. "So peanut butter is his Kryptonite, huh?"

"Now he's Superman? I thought he was the Terminator."

"You hang onto things way too long," Carson said. "Let it go."

"I'm just trying to follow your twisted train of thought."

"Don't try to keep up with me, kid. You can't."

He gave Marty a high wattage smile with just a hint of *fuck you* in it. "Now how are you going to get him to eat the peanut butter?"

"What's his favorite drink?"

"Huh?" The non-sequitur threw Carson for a second.

"Tanner. What is his favorite drink?"

This one Carson did know. Most of the time, Tanner drank whatever the client liked. Whenever it was just the two of them, they used to drink old fashioneds. But if it was just a casual drink with friends and Tanner wanted to savor something, he always ordered the same thing. "That's easy. Hot buttered rum."

"Exactly. He's mad for it."

Carson shrugged. *Mad for it* was a typically pretentious Marty way of putting it, but Tanner definitely loved his HBRs. "What's the point?"

"The point is, if he thinks he's getting hot buttered rum, he'll want it. And if he gets peanut butter instead…"

Carson thought about it. "Okayyyy… but how?"

Marty grinned like a Bond villain. "He's giving a speech at a charity event the day after tomorrow. I know the caterer."

"How?"

"She's married to another accountant."

"So, what? I don't see . . ."

"She makes a sweet concoction called HBR Surprise," Marty explained. "It's a pastry, a doughy hot buttered rum ball with a peanut butter center."

Carson's immediate reaction was to smile at the thought of Tanner choking to death. He gave Marty a grudging nod of admiration. "Not bad. How do you make sure he eats one?"

Marty's evil smile broadened. "I let the caterer know how much Tanner loves HBR. His wife is super-ambitious. She wants to impress him and get all those great referrals for other events. And once Tanner finds out they're hot buttered rum balls, he won't be able to resist popping one in his mouth."

That might work. Carson thought.

"It won't work," he said.

"Of course it will."

Carson frowned disapprovingly. "It's too complicated, just like everything you do."

"It's straightforward."

"No, it's not. How many things have to line up for it to work?"

"One," Marty insisted. "He has to eat a rum ball."

"No," Carson said. "You have to hope your buddy's wife decides to make the rum ball—"

"It's her specialty. And I told you, I already talked to her. She told me she's making it."

Carson ignored him and continued. "Then you have to hope the treat ends up in Tanner's orbit somehow, and that he decides to eat one, and that he doesn't get warned about the peanut butter middle, or smell it when he picks one up, and—"

"You're just shitting on the plan because it isn't yours."

"I'm pointing out that it sucks. It relies on too many factors you can't control." Carson meant what he said, though he greatly exaggerated how difficult he thought the obstacles were. In reality, this had a pretty good shot of succeeding. If he was betting on this, his money would be on Marty.

But he had a different play in mind, and that changed the odds.

"You'll be singing a different tune when Tanner chokes to death in front of five hundred people in tuxedos and black dresses," Marty told him.

"Maybe," Carson conceded. "I guess I'll have to make sure I'm there to see it happen."

Or to see it not *happen,* he thought to himself. Because a plan of his own was already starting to take shape. If it worked, Marty would fail and he would get the chance he should have gotten from the very beginning.

The chance to kill Tanner-goddamn-Fritz.

Chapter Twenty-Two

Barry

Barry and Lena had made love three times over the past two days and were planning on going for three squared as soon as the hour hand touched five. He'd finally found a vessel for all the years of built up libido and Lena, the lucky gal, was happy to absorb every last ounce of his affection.

She was an odd bird, to be sure, but she was genuine and pulled no punches, traits he liked. Everyone had been tiptoeing around his infirmities for years, afraid of insulting him or being embarrassed.

There was none of that with Lena—she spoke her mind unconditionally. And the sex, the sex was off the charts. She was an animal between the sheets. He was amazed that he was able to keep up with her, yet somehow he did. Moreover, she stood by him, against unfeeling Carson with his nasty mouth and anyone else who had something to say about her man.

Barry was sleeping better, eating with gusto, and had the sex drive of a three-balled Billy goat. He was stuttering less and was more confident than he thought possible.

He was thinking about her when Siegelman walked up to him, pouting and carrying his laptop. It was almost five. Nothing on hell or earth was going to make him late for Lena's bed. He channeled her mojo when he addressed his coworker. "The hell do you w-want, *Beagle*man?"

Siegelman's expression said, "Really?"

"What's with the p-puss?"

"What's with the name calling? Do you have a problem with my name?"

"No. I-I have a problem with you making me late."

"Late for what?"

"That's *my* business."

"Geez, what crawled up your ass and died, Barry?"

"You did. Now, are y-you going to tell me what you n-need or what?"

Siegelman started for the door. "Screw you, Barry. I'd rather pull an all-nighter and rewrite the whole fucking program than take advice from you now. Jesus, man, what the hell happened to you? You used to be a nice guy."

"T-that was before a w-wall of cloud servers came down on me like a g-goddamn avalanche."

"That was years ago, man. Get over it."

It took Barry a moment for the sting to subside. He looked up and reached for Siegelman's laptop. "Let me take a look."

"No fucking way, man. I don't need charity."

"I'm-I'm sorry."

Siegelman stopped walking and glanced over his shoulder.

"I've had a lot on my mind," Barry explained "W-what are you having a problem with?"

"This new security protocol," Siegelman said petulantly. "It hangs up and freezes. I can't get it to execute smoothly."

Barry held out his hand for the laptop but Siegelman held fast and shook his head.

"I-I apologized, didn't I?"

"Inadequate, woefully inadequate. What's my name, jerk?

"Siegelman, okay? Now let me take a look. You're here for help, aren't you?

"I was but you're not the only fish in the sea, Barry."

"I-I know." He kept his hands out with an upturned palm, submissively. "Can I take a look, please?"

Siegelman reluctantly acquiesced, returning and handing the laptop to him.

Barry flipped it open and began scanning the code with his face no more than a few inches from the screen.

"Your eyes going bad or something?"

"Just focusing. Looking close." He set the computer down on his lap and entered a few keystrokes, then picked it up and stared at the screen even more closely. "Eighty-one t-times."

"What are you talking about?" Siegelman looked over Barry's shoulder.

"This line." Barry underscored a line of highlighted code with his finger. "I did a search-and-find routine. You copy-paste this into the code?"

"I guess. Yeah, why? Don't you copy-paste code

to save time?"

"Y-yes, but you pasted it eighty-one times. Repetitive. Inefficient. You don't need it. Loop. Use loops instead, and this part . . ."

"Yeah?"

"Look—bad variable name and because you pasted it, you re-repeated it eighty-one times."

Siegelman turned red and snatched his laptop from Barry. "Thanks for nothing, man." He hurried out the door.

"Lamebrain," Barry mumbled as he began to pack up his gear. "Bush leaguer. Ought to be ashamed."

Barry didn't leave the building as early as he had hoped. Serena waylaid him on his way to the elevator after he helped Siegelman.

"What's going on, Barry?" She was all fired up.

"What do you mean?"

"Siegelman just tore into my office and went off like an artillery shell. He said he came to you for some help and you chewed him out over nothing."

"N-nothing? He-he's a dummy. We pay him a big sal-salary and he made a stupid mistake."

"He said you insulted him—made fun of his name. Said you're anti-Semitic."

Barry's face grew flush. "That's b-b-bullshit. My ex-wife was Jewish."

"You've got a lot of explaining to do. He made such a fuss that Tanner overheard him and came into my office. He's waiting for you downstairs in the parking lot. He wants to see you before he heads out." She checked her watch and called for the elevator. "Something is going on with you, Barry. You're not the same since you started dating that waitress."

Barry's eyes narrowed. "How do y-y-you know about her?"

"You told me," she said.

Did I? Barry tried to remember.

"She might not be good for you," Serena said. "I think she's gotten into your head."

"Don't care what you think," he snapped. "You let Carson into your pants."

"Lower your voice," she said as she checked to see if anyone was within earshot. "This isn't about me. I'm not the one losing control at work." The elevator door yawned open. "Better hustle your ass downstairs and be careful what you say. Tanner's been acting nervous lately. Don't say anything that gives him any ideas about you know what."

Barry stepped onto the elevator. "D-don't get your panties in a bunch," he said.

Serena watched him flatly as the door slid closed.

Down in the lobby, Barry headed out the door and made straight for the yellow Lamborghini under a full head of steam. Tanner was seated within, eyes closed, moving his hand like an orchestra conductor. He jumped when Barry rapped on the window and blew out a chest full of air before signaling for Barry to get into the car.

He mouthed, "Me?" leaving no doubt he was shocked that Tanner would allow him to defile his exotic automobile.

Tanner nodded.

Hesitantly, Barry walked around to the passenger side of the car to get in.

"You startled me, pal," Tanner said as Barry settled in and the scissor door closed. He reached for the volume control and lowered the sound a skosh. "Do you like Malagueña, Barry?"

"Mal-a-what? No. Never heard of it."

"You should give it a try. It's so... powerful. That's what I'd call it, powerful."

"I like t-t-the Stones. And Pearl J-j-jam"

"Sure, me, too. But this, Barry, it'll touch your soul."

"You want to bawl me out you-you'd better get started. I've got a date."

"A date?" Tanner patted him on the shoulder. "Atta boy. I'm glad to hear it. Anyone I know?"

"No. No one you know."

"Well, have a good time, but... listen, are we overworking you, sport? Are you feeling too much pressure?"

Barry shook his head.

Tanner lowered the music until it was mere background. "This row you had with Siegelman, it's so unlike you. And what troubles me most is that it's not the first complaint I've received. I've known you a long time, Barry. Is there something I can do to help?"

You can go back in time and take the precautions I begged you to take. You can give me my goddamn life back.

"N-no. I've got it under control."

"Do you, Barry? Do you have it under control? I know Siegelman's a whiner but he's saying you're a racist and that's a powerful allegation. We're going to have to investigate thoroughly. I'd like to help you smooth it over but when someone pulls the prejudice card... well, there's only so much I can do. And if it's true..."

"He's full of shit. I just made a little f-fun of his name. That's all. I'm as t-t-tolerant as they come."

"I always thought you were, but... look, my friend, can you tread lightly? Can you ease up on the staff? Let them know that you're there to help. And maybe bring Siegelman a basket of muffins. Mend some fences, would you? It couldn't hurt. Maybe he'll back off."

"I'm t-telling you, Tanner, this is all BS from a second-rate programmer."

"I'm just asking if you could take the high road from now on ... *please?*"

Barry grinned at him. It was the phoniest grin he'd ever given anyone and it felt good to know he was bullshitting the man who had taken so much from him. "S-sure, Tanner, I'll bury the hatchet."

Right in your neck.

Chapter Twenty-Three

Carson

This guy isn't buying, Carson had thought.

Fifteen minutes ago, he would have bet a thousand bucks on it. Now he had nearly that coming in commission as the customer in tattered jeans and a faded sweatshirt endured the process of signing the sales paperwork.

Carson hovered while Alice went through the transaction. He'd managed to avoid raising his eyebrows at the man's credit score, which was at least three hundred points higher than he'd have guessed. When he wrote out a check for the total amount instead of financing, Carson had to admit he'd judged a book by its cover and been wrong. Sure, the man had talked him down more than he'd expected, and yeah, he'd actually get a better commission if the man financed the vehicle through the dealership's loan division, but neither of those were the point. It was simply damn impressive to see anyone lay out full price for a quality automobile. When the guy who did it dressed like an unemployed failure to launch, who still lived with his parents, it was double-damn impressive.

He distracted the customer with sports talk while they waited for Alice to verify the funds. The man was amiable enough, but didn't seem to have strong opinions about any of the local teams. This surprised Carson a little, since the faded sweatshirt bore the logo of the state college. He probed a little for the man's interests and got another surprise.

"I'm interested in a lot of things," he said. "I'm a writer, so I pay attention to all sorts of subjects. But mostly, I watch people."

"People, huh? So you write for a magazine, or what?"

"I write science fiction novels."

Carson didn't know what to say to that. He'd met journalists and some movie writers, but no book writers. And he wasn't entirely certain what science fiction was. Finally, he stammered out, "Like, uh, Star Wars?"

The man gave a polite smile. "Same genre, yes. But very different. My work is more grounded in actual science."

Carson didn't have a suave answer to that, either, so he went to his go-to reply. He grinned and said, "Cool."

Alice came to his rescue. She got Mr. Book Man's attention, coaxed a few final signatures from him, and provided him with a packet of paperwork. Carson followed up, presenting the keys with great flourish.

"Your space ship awaits," he said. He made some *pew-pew* laser gun sounds while forming a gun with his thumb and forefinger.

Mr. Book Man accepted the keys graciously, but Carson thought he saw a hint of disdain from him. Oh, well. Nerds had never liked him much. At least this one was getting him a commission, and probably keeping him from getting transferred to the used car lot next week. He couldn't imagine what reject loaner car he'd have to drive to and from work if *that* happened.

After the transaction wrapped, he swung back around to Alice's desk. "Nice work," he told her.

She gave him a mixed expression of confusion and appreciation, blushing slightly. "It was nothing. A standard sale."

"No," Carson assured her. "I needed that sale, and you saved me back there. Talking to nerds is not my strong suit."

Alice smiled uncomfortably. "You've never read his books?"

"Have you?"

"Sure. He's really good."

Carson pursed his lips. "Really?"

"They've got everything," Alice continued. "Great characters, some action, some philosophy. Even a little… romance." She glanced away at the last word.

"Did they ever make a movie out of them?" Carson asked.

That brought Alice's gaze back to his. "Oh my god, I wish they would."

So they can't be that *good*, Carson thought. Any book worth a damn got made into a movie. Everyone knew that.

"Well, if they ever do," Carson said, "we should go see it."

Alice's eyes widened slightly. "That'd be great," she whispered. "I'd like that."

"Me, too." Carson smiled winningly, knowing the hook was already set. "But why wait until then? I've got tickets to this charity event tomorrow night. Maybe you'd like to be my plus one?"

"*Really*? I'd love to," Alice gushed.

Of course you would. Carson wondered how much work he'd need to put into this date to make it work. Given her reaction, he was betting a C+ effort would get the job done.

"What's the charity?" she asked.

"Huh?"

"The event? What's the charity?"

"Oh." Carson realized he didn't know. "I'm not really sure," he admitted. "It's one my old business partner supports. I'm just supporting him, you know?"

"Tanner Fritz?" she asked.

He forced himself to smile bigger. "That's him."

"I thought you hated him."

Carson's smile faltered. "What? No. Why would you say that?"

"It's just that in the break room a couple weeks ago, you said something."

"You must have misunderstood. What did I say?"

"You said, 'Tanner-goddamn-Fritz. I hate that guy.' You were talking to Stu."

Shit.

He audibled. "Well, that explains it. I only said that because Stu hates him."

"Stu knows Tanner Fritz?"

"I guess so. He hates the guy." Carson powered past the point. "So I'll pick you up around seven?"

The thought of her date with Carson seemed to

push everything else aside. She blushed again. "Sounds great. I'll text you my address."

"Perfect." Carson grinned. Then he squatted down and scratched Alice's therapy dog on the head. "And make sure this guy comes along, too, huh?"

"*She* goes with me everywhere," Alice said, frowning slightly.

"She," Carson repeated. Then he remembered the dog's name. "Of course. Merlot, right?"

Alice nodded, her expression still mixed.

"Well, see you both tomorrow night," Carson said, amping up the wattage on his smile to the maximum. "I can't wait."

As he walked away, his own smile faded, but only a little. He congratulated himself on his plan. All it was going to take to foil Marty's attempt on Tanner was a couple of girls he'd bring to the party.

Chapter Twenty-Four

Serena

For as long as she'd lived in the building, the sanitation truck had reliably picked up the garbage at six a.m. every Tuesday and Thursday morning. She stuffed her soiled clothes into a black plastic trash bag. Rolled into a ball, the items were small, microfiber and Spandex garments that were practically shed resistant. Her sneakers were women's Converse with a common sole pattern. Still, they went into the bag along with the other garments. She sealed the items, then double-bagged them before slipping into sweats, hustling downstairs, and stuffing the bag into a refuse can.

It was about two in the morning but she was too worked up to sleep and decided to take a bath—just her, a tub of warm soapy water, and a bottle of Coppola Rosso. A good soak always made her sleepy. The wine was the kicker. It was like slugging a bottle of ZzzQuil.

She finally felt good about the situation. She was taking matters into her own hands, returning control to the only one of the four with the experience and acumen to put Tanner down cleanly and permanently.

"The guys," she snickered. They were amusing, in

their own fashion, as long as they didn't get caught. Barry and his trailer park floozy, legend-in-his-own-mind Carson, and Marty, the bean counter. They were all lightweights in the end. Together they couldn't kill a six-pack of Budweiser.

In cahoots with Lena, Barry had successfully assassinated a fire hydrant and a pair of very expensive, surgically implanted silicone prosthetics. As a murder weapon they had cleverly employed the same junkyard truck the Beverly Hillbillies had used to transport their worldly possessions to California from their shack in the Ozarks.

She visualized the *hit*, and snorted in laughter. "What were those idiots thinking?" True, their vehicle wasn't flashy and it was unregistered, but it was such a unique car. *The police would've nailed them in two seconds flat if they'd decided to utilize their resources.* A little canvassing was all it would take, a few days of going door-to-door asking, "Have you seen anyone behind the wheel of the truck Jed Clampett used to drive?"

Luckily that kind of police work didn't go into no-injury-hit and-runs.

Marty the accountant was up next, a man whose biggest risk in life was switching brands of No. 2 pencils. She'd been cultivating that particular psychological quirk before Andrea swooped in and spoiled things. Behind his back, Carson used to call Marty the little engine that couldn't, and Serena was inclined to agree with him these days.

"This is the guy who's going to put Tanner's lights out? *Puhhh.*" The puff of air left her lips in disdain. She had no idea how Marty planned to execute his hit. *Maybe he'll wish him dead. That's about Marty's speed.*

She didn't know how it would play out, but she could easily guess the result. Like most things in his life, Marty would quietly fail.

And then there was Carson, God's gift to the world, the man who felt that he was above everyone. He was the best racquetball player, the best car salesman, the best drinker, the best lay, the best, the best, the best. The word *modesty* wasn't in his vocabulary.

Overconfident to the extreme, even more so to compensate once he suffered some setbacks, he lauded his superiority over anyone foolish enough to listen to him. Of course his plan was going to succeed. He was Carson, after all. The possibility of failure never crossed his mind.

She wondered how a tool like Carson might attempt to kill Tanner. She sipped her wine and gave it a good ponder. *A guy like Carson, he's got to do something macho that would out Tanner for who he really was.* Not just a dick but a super dick, the guy who hobbled one of his best friends, stole the wife of another, and swindled millions from a third.

Tanner's execution had to come in a way for Carson to show himself superior to Tanner—perhaps a duel at twenty paces. Of course Carson would be armed with a modern day assault rifle and Tanner with a muzzle-loading blunderbuss. That was Carson's notion of fairness—he'd always deserved the high ground. He was overconfident to a fault.

She refilled her glass and enjoyed the wine as it

lapped on her tongue. "Knock yourself out, Marty," she said aloud. "You, too, Carson. And after the two of you blow it . . ." She sank deeper into the tub with a sigh, letting the last ounce of tension from her tired muscles seep into the bath water. "Then, baby, watch out because it's my fucking turn."

Chapter Twenty-Five

Barry

All the newly found confidence that was growing within Barry manifested itself when he stood before the mirror opining on his appearance in a rented tux. Tanner's charity event had arrived and he wasn't going to miss it for the world. It didn't bother him that Marty was going to have the honor of ending the prick. The important thing was that he got what he deserved. Tanner was going to die.

He glanced over at his phone, wondering if perhaps he'd missed a call from Lena. She was going with him as his guest. They had planned for her to meet him at the event after she got off from work at the diner. He was eager to see her again, even though it'd only been since last night that he'd seen her last.

Leaping Judas, I'm acting like a lovesick fifteen-year-old.

Even so, he reached for the phone and checked for messages. Nothing. No text, no voicemail, no missed call. That was odd, since she'd begun teasing him right out of the box, sending him provocative innuendos throughout most days: messages left in a sultry voice, suggestive text messages, and tit pics in front of a shelf filled with cleaning supplies in the diner closet, right near the booth where they'd sat on what Barry now considered their first date.

But for some reason he hadn't heard from her all day and now he worried that he knew why.

She was trying to back out.

She has to show, he fretted. He had to show the world that he had a date. Not just a date but a hot date, a blonde who couldn't keep her hands off him.

Her unexplained silence grated on his nerves. He'd played it out in his mind, showing Lena off during the event and ending the night by watching Tanner meet his maker. What a spectacular evening it would be. He picked up his phone and rang her again. She was usually quick to answer with a witty barb but the call went to voicemail and her mailbox was full.

"W-what the hell is going on?" he muttered after terminating the call. He checked his bowtie in the mirror. He'd at first thought it was even and perfect but now felt differently. He pulled on one end, undoing it, and started again from scratch. This time, however, perfection was more elusive. He tied and untied it several times without satisfaction. He finally gave up, exhausted, the untied end hanging to the middle of his chest.

He called once more.

Nothing.

He texted, *I'm worried about you. Please call me right away. You're still going with me, right?* He waited five minutes for a response but none came.

Barry checked his watch. It was a half hour before her shift ended and although they had planned to meet at the venue… He gathered his phone and wallet and rushed out the door. "G-g-goddamn it," he said and dashed off. He wasn't going to let his big day wither on the vine.

He hailed a cab and was on his way to the diner.

Chapter Twenty-Six

Carson

"Wow," Alice said breathlessly. "This place is nice."

Carson glanced around. The hotel ballroom looked like every other he'd ever been to for events like these. There was a small stage at the front of the room with a podium and a microphone. Plenty of open space for milling about and networking between the scattered round tables where the audience could sit to eat and fawn over Tanner. To his mind, once a certain level of quality was achieved with regard to the location, it stopped being a factor. So did the purpose of the event. People were the point, and schmoozing was the goal.

"Where are our seats?" Alice asked. She kept her therapy dog's leash short, but it seemed like a needless precaution. Carson was amazed at how calm the animal was, and how much it didn't react to the people around it. He'd seen the affection it gave Alice on occasion at the office, during her coffee breaks and lunchtimes. He wondered how the animal could have such an on/off switch. Training, he supposed. Still, if a hunk of prime rib floated by, the dog would have to eat it, right?

"It's open seating," Carson told her. "But I know

where the best seats are." He flashed a grin.

Alice smiled back, still glowing at the attention from him. He noticed she wasn't blushing anymore, though. Already getting used to life in Carson's sunshine.

Roughly half of the people in the ballroom were already seated, but Carson saw from across the room that the pair of open seats he'd reserved near the back remained empty. *Reserved* was a fancy word for what he'd done, which was to slip in hours ago and place a large printed card on each that read Reserved on the table in front of the two seats he wanted.

The simpler a plan is, the better chance it'll work, he thought. Which was why Marty's plan was doomed to fail.

He grabbed Alice by the hand and led her through the milling crowd toward the seats. He tried to take a route that avoided anyone from his days at Chismo, which quickly proved difficult. So he plastered on his million-dollar smile, and gave a quick nod to anyone who recognized him, then looked away to the next person before that previous eye contact could evolve into an hello, or God forbid, a conversation.

Along the way, he spotted Marty standing along the wall in the back corner, shoulders slumping. The little man looked like a bug about to be squashed. He was staring at the front of the room, and didn't notice Carson.

They arrived at their seats near the back, and Carson gathered up the Reserved cards, folded them, and slipped them under his chair.

"You reserved these seats?" she asked.

"Best seats in the house," he proclaimed.

"But I thought you said this was open seating."

"I know a guy," he said. He gave her a quick eyebrow raise to go with his smile. Then he gestured grandly with his arm toward the seat nearest a nearby door. "Your seat, my lady."

Alice grinned like a fool and settled into the chair. Her dog sat without being told. Carson stood next to her, not sitting just yet. Instead, he surveyed the room. Despite the fact that there were a fair number of people that he knew, he was a little surprised at how many he didn't. A lot had changed in two years. He supposed that worked to his advantage, though—fewer awkward conversations. Sitting at the rear of the ballroom provided an additional advantage where that was concerned.

Still, it bothered him that there was a buzz in the room and he wasn't part of it. He was in his element, and should be slipping from group to group, handshake to back slap, not just being part of the buzz, but creating it. Once Tanner bought him out, though, that ceased to happen in these circles. Despite his departure, they all seemed to be able to continue on just fine without him.

That sucked.

He found Marty along the wall again. His friend was still staring at the front of the room.

Carson followed his gaze. At first, he thought Marty was looking at the open podium and the easel up on a makeshift stage, where Tanner Fritz would be making his little speech, trying to pry money out of all these people for . . . for what, again?

He narrowed his eyes slightly, reading the oversized poster board on the easel. Children's Cancer Care Raffle! He stopped reading after that, remembering. This had long been Tanner's pet charity, even back when Chismo was barely scratching out a profit. Carson remembered it had something to do with his younger brother dying of cancer when the two were still kids. Tanner said he had survivor's guilt, but Carson imagined that he was just using the family tragedy as a way to tug on heartstrings and rack up some more donations, all of which made Chismo look better in the public eye. Which, of course, didn't hurt sales one iota.

Bottom line, baby. It's all about the bottom line.

But why would Marty be staring at that?

Carson looked back to Marty again, following his gaze more carefully. Then he saw the object of Marty's attention.

Andrea.

She sat at the front table, the one nearest the podium. Right where she could be the last person Tanner interacted with before going on stage. The doting husband—great for the good-guy image.

Carson could see why Marty was hung up on Andrea. She was still a stunner. Dressed in an off-white number that showed her bare shoulders, she sat with her shapely legs crossed, chatting with some bigwig seated next to her.

Stitch married waaaaaaaaaay above his station with that one. How he managed it in the first place was a mystery to Carson, but now that she was with an alpha male again, the natural order had been re-established. Marty should just accept it and find himself a woman at his own level.

Like Alice here, he thought. Hell, maybe he should introduce the two of them. Although now that Alice had been out with him, Carson wondered if she'd ever be satisfied by a beta male like Marty. Well, she better get used to the idea, because after tonight, the most she was getting from him was some sales paperwork.

"Who's that?" Alice asked, breaking into his reverie.

"Huh?" Carson glanced down at her.

"The woman you're looking at." Her voice was a little tight. She didn't exactly sound jealous, but then again, she didn't sound *not* jealous, either. Carson didn't really care either way but he knew he had to keep her happy for a little while longer.

"An old college friend," he said. "Her name is Andrea. She used to be married to another friend of mine but now she's married to Tanner."

Alice appeared to relax a little.

So she *had* been jealous.

"Well, she's really pretty."

"Yes," Carson agreed. Then he turned to her. "She might even be the second-most beautiful woman in the room."

That got her to blush again, and Carson upped the ante by giving her a sly wink.

That should about do it, he figured.

"Listen," he said. "My other friend, the one who used to be married to her? Well, he's here, and without a date. I can tell from across the room that he's bumming about it. I need to slip over there and make him feel a little better, okay? I'll be back before you know it."

"All right," Alice said.

Carson pointed to the nearby door. "Remember when I said these were the best seats in the house? Well, here's why. Tanner Fritz is going to come through that door in a few minutes. You'll get an up-close view of why people think he's such a rock star."

"And why people like Stu hate him?" Alice asked.

"Exactly." Carson cocked his thumb and dropped it, pointing his finger at her and making a *click* out of the corner of his mouth. "Be right back."

He turned and made his way toward Marty, who had chosen a spot almost exactly in the back corner. As he approached, he wondered how long it would take his friend to notice him. He appeared very intent on watching Andrea.

This was going to be great. Not only would he get to watch Marty's plan go down in flames, thanks to his own brilliant scheme, but he'd do it while standing right next to the guy. He couldn't wait to see Marty's jaw drop.

He made it all the way to Marty without having to chat with anyone, and without Marty noticing him. He sidled up next to the smaller man, leaning back against the wall.

"Hey, Stitch," he said.

Marty turned, and gave him a look of surprise. Carson was betting it wasn't going to be the last time he saw that look tonight.

Chapter Twenty-Seven

Barry

Barry's finger was raw and bloody—he'd chewed it down to the nub. Lena was a no-show to work—no call-out, no nothing. She simply didn't report—first time ever. Her boss explained that she'd always been reliable and was more worried than angry. He said that he tried calling her but her mailbox was full.

He washed his hands in the men's room and wrapped a linen towelette around his bloody fingertip. It didn't take much to stop it but when his phone buzzed he jammed his hand into his pocket hopeful that Lena was finally trying to make contact. His finger bled worse than before and his annoyance was further compounded when he saw that the text was not from Lena but from the motherfucker himself, Tanner Fritz, asking Barry to join him in the green room at the charity event as soon as possible.

"Son of a bitch!" He'd been balancing on the point of a spire all day and now felt himself beginning to slip. Looking down from a towering height he saw the abyss below and the inevitability of a mental collapse. It was Lena's affection and lust that had propped him up and without her to hold him up the plunge seemed imminent.

A second message from Tanner set him in motion. *Tight schedule. Please hurry.*

He wrapped his finger in a fresh towelette and hurried out the door.

Barry knocked on the green room door, waited for Tanner's acknowledgment, then entered.

Tanner was the picture of elegance in his bespoke tuxedo, legs crossed as he sat, sipping champagne, and reading an index card, mouthing the words to his forthcoming speech.

Barry was shaking, his left eye twitching as he unwound the towelette and stuffed it into his pocket. "Y-y-you wanted to see m-me?"

"My God, man, are you all right?" Tanner asked, getting immediately to his feet and crossing the room. "I've never seen you so nervous." He placed a comforting hand on Barry's shoulder. "Can I get you a drink? Something to settle your nerves?"

"N-no thanks. I'll, I'll, I'll be okay."

Tanner seemed strained. "I'm worried about you, Barry. You haven't been yourself. Sit down, will you? Take a deep breath—relax."

Barry took his advice. He breathed in deeply, then slowly exhaled.

"That's it," Tanner said. "Just breathe." His voice took on a dreamy quality while he patted Barry on the shoulder. "I have to remember to slow down and breathe myself sometimes. All the hustle of the business can be overwhelming, especially these last two years since the acquisition. That's why it feels good to be involved in a charity like this one. There's no pressure, just a chance to give back."

"K-k-kids with cancer, right?"

Tanner nodded, his expression mournful. "My little brother died from Ewing's sarcoma when we were kids. Did you know that?"

Barry shook his head. "N-n-no. S-s-so, that's why the charity?"

"That's why *this* charity," Tanner said. "If it helps save just one child from the pain my little brother went through..." His voice trailed off momentarily, then he shook himself from the trance. "Sorry about that. I asked you here to talk about you, not me or my brother."

"No problem. W-w-what's up?"

Tanner settled into his original chair. He reached for a round doughy ball on a nearby platter, picking one up but not eating it. "Look, my friend, we go back a long way. Hell, since college, right?"

"Sophomore year. W-why?" His gnawed finger was oozing onto his rental pants. He slipped his hand into his pants pocket but it was an uncomfortable position. He ended up tucking his hand under his leg.

Tanner cocked his head. It looked as if he was searching his memory. "Right, student union building—we started off talking politics and wound up in my dorm room smoking pot with my roommate. What was his name?" Tanner shook his head. "Talk about a stoner, I don't have a single memory of him being straight."

Barry grunted. He couldn't remember the day Tanner mentioned. Whenever he thought of college, it was always the five of them together the Thanksgiving of their senior year. Giving the finger to their families and staying at school to be with each other. Since the accident, though, those memories seemed more and more like they belonged to someone else.

Tanner fidgeted in his seat before looking Barry in the eye. Instead, he stared down at the small pastry in his fingers. Then he placed it back on the corner of the tray. "Look, Barry, this is hard for me to say but Siegelman's complaint hit corporate headquarters this morning. Santo Corp has a strict policy and HR flat out told me that I had to terminate you."

Barry cringed. "Oh, *shit*." He buried his face in his hands. "I'm n-n-not having a great day."

Tanner stood and poured him a glass of water. "Hold on—Serena and I were able to negotiate a stay of execution, but it comes with conditions." He handed him the glass.

Barry took a sip but had trouble forcing it down his throat. "What k-kind of conditions?"

"No more roaming. They insisted that you be moved to a position without direct employee-to-employee contact. Coders will write up their issues and send them into a blind mailbox. The queries and your responses will be anonymous."

His face lost all color. "Will I have to, to stay in an office? You know I-I-I can't."

"Farther removed than that, I'm afraid. Your new position is remote."

"R-remote?"

"Yes. I know you can't be confined and that's why I went to bat for you. I felt I owed you that." Tanner grew quiet for a moment, then said. "Because of the accident, I mean. I handled the hardware move on a shoestring instead of going with your recommendation. I'm sorry, Barry."

Barry tried to remember if he'd ever heard those words come from Tanner before. Maybe he'd said it when Barry was still unconscious, or during his recovery, when all he could concentrate on was the most basic of needs. But since he'd come back to work?

Never.

"That was a tense time." Tanner's voice sounded a little thick. "I'd just bought out Carson a few weeks before and Santo Corp started sniffing around, but they weren't going to buy unless we jumped through certain hoops. I needed three dollars for every dollar I had in order to get that done, but I had to find a way to make it work somehow, Barry. The amount of money they were offering to buy us up was life-changing."

Life-changing? Barry ground his teeth. Yes, it had been.

"Anyway," Tanner said, clearing his throat. "I cashed in all the favors I had at corporate to swing this arrangement. I'm just glad they went for it."

"Thanks . . . thanks," Barry stammered. "Tanner. I—"

"You owe me? No, we're even. Or as close as we can ever get. But it's the last thing I can do for you. Serena's been getting almost daily complaints from your colleagues. Whatever it is you're going through has to stop because if it doesn't . . ." Tanner sighed. "The next stop is the unemployment line. No more chances. I've got no more favors to call in. Do we

No Dibs On Murder

understand each other?"

"Yes. But working remotely I-I won't be in a position to-to get in trouble."

"By design, yes. You can work from home, Starbucks, the beach—your choice. Anywhere you can establish a connection via secure VPN."

Barry thought about it. The set up didn't sound that bad, especially compared to the prospect of being fired. The divorce settlement had left him on the short side of solvency, living paycheck to paycheck. The reaction from his former peers would be bad, too, but the idea of having to interview for another job somewhere else terrified him.

"So, are we in agreement?" Tanner extended his hand and Barry took it.

"Deal," Barry said. Now he felt a pang of regret for trying to run Tanner over in Lena's truck. That made him think of her again, and his bloody finger twitched in response. He swallowed thickly. "I'm n-n-not gonna look a gift horse in the m-m-mouth."

A torrent of air whooshed from Tanner's lungs. "Good." He glanced at a tray of glistening rum balls. "I've been fighting the urge to devour one of these for the last thirty minutes. But my stomach's been a mess lately, and besides they're about twelve hundred calories apiece." He extended the tray toward Barry. "You like hot buttered rum balls, don't you? I'm mad for them. Can't just eat one of them, know what I mean?"

Barry nervously took one and popped it in his mouth.

"As good as it looks?" Tanner asked.

Barry rolled it around his mouth until his saliva

became thick with sweetness. The doughy concoction tasted just like a hot buttered rum drink, minus the bite of alcohol. He bit down and his mouth flooded with the taste of peanut butter.

Oh shit! Peanuts were Tanner's Achilles heel. *If he eats this . . .?*

Barry's eyes opened wide. *Marty*! *Marty did this.*

"That good?" Tanner asked.

In that moment, a thousand thoughts ran through Barry's mind. The feeling of gratitude nudged him in one direction, but the image of a falling server pushed him the other. Lena's inexplicable silence sealed it for him. "Uh-huh," he said around the doughy ball in his mouth. "Special, r-r-really special, Tanner."

"That's all the twisting my arm needs." He was reaching for one when someone knocked on the door.

A brunette in an evening gown poked in her head, smiling warmly. "We're ready for you, Mr. Fritz."

"Shoot," Tanner said with a look of disappointment. He grabbed a treat anyway. "One for the road. It's a long walk to the podium."

Eat that and you'll never make it there, Barry thought.

Tanner stepped in front of a mirror and checked his appearance. "Show time, Barry. Got to go."

Chapter Twenty-Eight

Marty

"What are you doing here?" Marty asked Carson.
"Supporting the fight against cancer."
"Bullshit."
Carson grinned. "Easy, Stitch. I just came to see the show."
Marty frowned. He hadn't expected Carson to come to this event. Carson didn't like being around Chismo employees if he could help it. Their presence reminded him too much of the money and status he'd lost.
And yet, here he was, standing next to him. More than that, smiling that way? Did he have something planned?
"Did you come with Serena?" he asked. If Serena were here, too, then he'd know something was up.
"No. She's been a little distant since . . . well, you know. Since our little project started." Carson pointed toward a table at the back of the ballroom, near the entrance that led to the green room. "No, I came with Alice."
Marty searched the seats near where he'd pointed. Then he spotted a woman with a therapy dog. "Alice from work?" He looked back at Carson. "You took Alice from work on a date?"

"Yeah."

"Alice the nerd?"

"Yeah."

"Alice, who you deride for needing a therapy dog?"

"Come on, Marty. I don't... wait, what's *deride* mean?"

"Tease. Cut down. Mock." Marty rattled off the synonyms. "All things you've done behind her back, and maybe some to her face. And you're taking *that girl* on a date?"

"Hey, nerds need love, too. Look at you."

Marty shook his head. "Even if you believed that, you'd never think you should be the one giving that love. What's going on?"

"Maybe I just realized she's a nice woman," Carson said. "Ever think of that?"

Marty gave him a dubious look.

"Maybe I just started talking to her, and it turns out she's nice. As in, not a bimbo."

Marty's skepticism didn't waver.

"Besides," Carson continued, "Serena has been giving me the cold shoulder the last few days, so maybe my confidence needed a boost."

Marty hesitated. He'd never known Carson to lack for confidence before. Although, he had been crushed when Santo Corp bought Chismo. That had been a low point for him, and Marty had to admit that behind his bravado, Carson had seemed decidedly insecure since then.

"You know, I'm not bulletproof, Stitch," Carson added.

Marty felt a pang of remorse for his suspicion.

Sometimes he forgot that beneath Carson's carefully manufactured persona was a real, breathing person with actual feelings.

"Sorry," he said, feeling shitty. "I just thought..."

"Yeah, I know what you thought. Don't worry about it."

Marty nodded his thanks. Then another thought struck him, along with renewed suspicion. "If she's your date, why aren't you sitting with her?"

Carson looked pained. "You were standing over here by yourself. I saw you staring at Andrea up in the front row."

"Oh." Marty's face reddened. "I was..."

"Staring," Carson finished. "I know. Anyway, I thought you could use a friend right about now. That you needed me. I've got the whole night to spend with Alice."

Now Marty felt double shitty. "I... uh, thanks, man."

"No problem. That's what friends are for. Emotional support and planning murder."

Marty looked around frantically at the people seated in the nearby chairs, but no one had heard Carson. The small distance between them and the buzz in the room deadened the words. Even so, he lowered his own voice before he spoke. "You can't say things like that. Especially not when we're near you-know-who."

"My bad," Carson said easily.

Marty tried to remember the last time Carson had accepted even a gentle rebuke from him. Usually, he snapped off a cutting comeback. Failing that, he lashed out with a punch in the arm or a cuff to the back of the head. Or at least the threat of one or the other. Instead, Carson simply leaned against the wall with that same, oddly content smile.

Stop being so suspicious. He's your friend. He knows how hard it is to be around Andrea, and he's trying to be supportive.

Marty returned the smile. It was good to have a friend at times like these.

The jostle of a microphone came over the speakers. Marty glanced to the podium to see a woman in an expensive gown leaning into the mic. He recognized her as Portia Dean, a board member for the children's cancer charity. Portia welcomed the crowd to the event, and paused to let the talking subside. She launched into a brief story about how she first met Tanner Fritz, and then detailed his involvement in the charity. This allowed people time to find their seats.

Marty barely listened to Portia extoll Tanner's virtues. Instead, he watched Andrea for a few moments, her face awash with happiness and pride. Her expression cut through his chest like a dull knife.

I don't love you. And I'm happy now.

He tore his eyes away from Andrea and to the back entrance. If things had gone right in the green room, Tanner had smelled Belinda's specialty, the hot buttered rum balls, and popped one in his mouth. Marty imagined the look of shock on his face when Tanner bit down and tasted the peanut butter. That shock would swiftly turn to terror when the allergy took hold. He could almost see Tanner spit out the doughy ball, but it wouldn't matter. In a few short moments, he'd be clawing at his throat as his

No Dibs On Murder

airways slammed shut. Terrible way to go, but it couldn't happen to a nicer guy.

He wasn't going to get to see it happen, of course. Still, he'd be able to observe all of the chaos when the medics arrived. The ensuing craziness of the crowd would keep him satisfied until the big moment came, when they wheeled Tanner out on a gurney. By then, Mister Perfect would be gonzo.

His eyes flicked back to Andrea, just for a moment. She'd need comfort right about then, wouldn't she? As they whisked Tanner away in an ambulance? It'd be a true crisis for her. And in times of crisis, what brought comfort more than something that was familiar? Or some*one* familiar?

Someone like him.

Marty stared at the rear door, waiting.

Portia Dean wrapped up her verbal love letter to Tanner Fritz with a question to the crowd. "But wouldn't you like to hear about this from the man himself?"

Enthusiastic applause erupted from the crowd.

"So would I," Portia said. "So without further ado, I give you one hell of a humanitarian... Tanner Fritz!"

The spotlight swung from Portia to the rear door.

A small, involuntary smile tugged at the corner of Marty's mouth. He relished the surprise they were all going to get.

Then the door swung open, and Tanner walked through. He took one step into the room and stopped, bathed in the spotlight and waved to the crowd.

Marty's face fell.

His plan had failed.

He gaped at Tanner as the man stood in the doorway and soaked in the crowd's adulation. His supreme magnetism shone outward. As he waved and smiled, it seemed as if he was waving and smiling to each individual there in the room. The faces near him seem to light up from that faux attention. The people nearest to Tanner, including Alice, were positively beaming.

This is Tanner Fritz, he thought. *Everyone loves him, and he gets everything. And it sucks.*

After the initial moment of shock, Marty realized Tanner was only waving with one hand. He seemed to be holding something in his other hand. Marty squinted to get a better look. When he identified what it was, a shot of adrenaline shot through him.

A hot buttered rum surprise.

Tanner was holding death in his hand.

Come on, you prick, Marty thought. *Stop smiling and eat it. You can chew on the way to the podium.*

In a flash, Marty decided that this was even better than his original plan. This way, Tanner would collapse in the aisle and choke to death in front of everyone in attendance. It would be epic.

Tanner stop waving. He took a step toward the podium, raising the rum ball to his mouth.

Marty felt himself grinning involuntarily, crazily.

Then Tanner noticed Alice's dog. He paused and smiled. "Look at that pretty boy," he said.

People nearby broke into *oohs* and laughter. Further away, some stood to get a look at the object of Tanner's attention. A smattering of applause came from others.

Alice, flushed with embarrassment, said something to Tanner as he started to move away, lifting the treat again. Marty couldn't hear but Tanner stopped and asked her to repeat herself. Then he said, "Oh, I'm sorry. It's a girl."

Alice blushed further.

The therapy dog sniffed at the rum ball. Tanner laughed and nudged it toward her. Merlot didn't need any further encouragement. She gobbled up the rum ball.

Marty was stricken. His jaw dropped.

Tanner gave Merlot a final pat, stood and smiled at Alice, and made his way toward the podium.

Marty stared at the dog, who was working her mouth from the peanut butter. A few moments later, he heard Tanner's booming "hello!" to the crowd and the rousing cheer in response.

"You're not supposed to pet a service animal," Marty muttered.

"Yeah," Carson said. "What the hell?"

Chapter Twenty-Nine

Carson

Once they assembled at Marty's apartment, Carson knew Marty was going to start a whine-fest. He'd expected it. Hell, he'd counted on it. What he hadn't realized was that his friend was going to make an Olympic sport out of it.

Carson followed the same strategy he'd always used, one he'd once heard originated with the CIA— *admit nothing, deny everything, and counter-accuse.* If it was good enough for James Bond, he figured it was good enough for him.

"You were only there to mess with things!" Marty yelled. "Admit it!"

Carson admitted nothing.

"You don't even *like* Alice. She was only there because of her dog."

"That's not true," Carson denied.

"You sabotaged my plan!"

"Maybe *you* sabotaged your plan," Carson counter-accused.

And so it went. Marty thrust, he parried. Carson enjoyed the exchange until Serena interrupted with a sharply.

"Enough!" She glared at Carson knowingly for a

moment, then cast her gaze on Marty. "It was a dumb plan, Marty."

"It would have worked," Marty whined, crestfallen. "If it weren't for Carson and that stupid therapy dog."

"Now you sound like a Scooby-Doo villain, right after the mask comes off."

Marty became quiet. The four of them sat in his sparsely furnished apartment in silence for a long while. Barry brooded, a worried expression on his face. Marty pouted angrily, refusing to even look at Carson. Serena waited impatiently, looked around at the rest of them with unveiled contempt. For his part, Carson reveled in his success. Maybe even gloated a little.

Once the silence had gone on long enough, he decided to move things along. "So, it's my turn," he pronounced.

That got Marty's attention. "You should have to forfeit your turn," he persisted. "For sabotaging mine."

Carson held up a finger. "One, no I didn't and B, even if I did, there's no clause that says anything about that. And three—"

"Of course there's no clause. There's no contract, you idiot."

"You tried to poison Tanner with a pastry treat, and *I'm* the idiot?"

"It would have worked if you hadn't—"

"If I hadn't what? Gone on a date?"

"You know what you did."

"I did nothing," Carson said. "Tanner's the one who decided to pet a service dog. You're not supposed to do that when they're working. Did you know that?"

Marty glowered at him.

Carson ignored him. "So, like I said, it's my turn. Are we agreed?"

"No!" Marty said vehemently.

Carson glanced at Barry, who was still off in la-la land. He turned away. "Serena?"

She gave him a bored, disdainful look. "Sure, stud. You're up."

Marty looked disconsolate. "Thanks for the support," he muttered, looking down at his feet.

Serena didn't reply.

"You had your chance, Stitch," Carson said. "Barry?"

Barry had been staring at his bandaged finger during the entire conversation. Now he looked up at Carson slowly, as if digesting the words. Finally, he said, "F-f-fine. Your turn."

Carson grinned widely. "Awesome."

"So what's your brilliant plan?" Marty snapped. "Hire Russian snipers?"

"I've thought about this," Carson began, "and I decided that I'm *not* going to try to run him down in the street or poison him with baked goods."

"Fuck you, Carson."

"Y-yeah, Carson. F-fuck you."

Carson raised his hands in a peaceful gesture. "Easy, guys. I'm just busting your balls."

Neither man appeared placated.

"Seriously," he said. "We're on the same team here."

He saw distrust and suspicion in their eyes. That

No Dibs On Murder

would have to change.

"Look, I need help on this one. I have a plan, but I need your expertise to get it to work. So this one will be a team effort, okay?" That was true, too. Of course, he'd be the lead.

The expressions on both of their faces softened a little, and that was enough of an opening for him. "Marty, you're a science guy, right?"

"I'm an accountant. How do you not know this?"

"I know you're an accountant—but you took all those science classes back in college, right? You know chemistry?"

"Not really. I took a couple science courses for my undergraduate requirements. Why?"

"I need you to mix up some plastic explosive for me."

"Uh, *what?*"

"You know, the play-dough looking stuff that explodes. I need some. But only a little."

"What makes you think I can just whip up a batch of C4?"

Carson snapped his fingers. "That's it. C4. See, you're smart, Marty. You can do this."

"No, I can't."

"I only need, like, this much." He mimed a piece the size of a pencil eraser.

"How much you need doesn't matter. I have no idea how to make—"

"Why do you want C4?" Serena interrupted.

Carson smiled his winningest smile. "I'm going to blow up his phone while it's pressed to his ear."

Serena frowned.

Marty groaned. "That'll never work."

"Sure, it will."

"It's too complex."

Carson looked at him sideways. "Says the pastry killer? *Your* plan was too complex. I even told you that, remember?"

"So is yours," Marty insisted. "There are too many variables."

"Such as?"

Marty shook his head, incredulous. "I don't even know where to begin."

"See?" Carson snapped his fingers. "It's simple. You whip up some C4, Serena steals Tanner's phone, and Barry here wires it to blow up at the time I choose. Then I make sure the phone is right up against Tanner's ear when it goes boom."

Now it was Serena's turn to groan.

"What?" Carson asked. "It could work."

"No, it can't," she said.

"See?"

Marty's superior tone irked him, but Serena's disapproval cut even deeper. Carson crossed his arms and looked away, shaking his head. "I would have helped any of you."

"What?"

In his peripheral vision, he saw Marty's jaw drop.

"I would have," he insisted, "if you'd asked me."

"That's such bullshit," Marty said, exasperated. "You literally –"

"I c-c-can do it," Barry said.

The other three stopped and turned their heads toward him, unbelieving.

"You can?" Carson asked.

"Yeah. N-n-not the stupid way you want, b-b-but

there's a way to get it done."

The three waited for Barry to explain. As he did, their expressions slowly shifted. First Carson, then Marty, and finally Serena, as disbelief turned to doubt and eventually to grudging approval.

When Barry had finished, Carson tilted his head. "They really have that kind of thing is on the 'net?"

"Everything is on the internet," Serena assured him. "It's not just porn. You just need to know where to look."

"Huh." Carson shrugged. "Okay, then. It's a plan."

"It still won't work, even with the elaborate set up," Marty said.

"Don't be a killjoy, Stitch. It'll work."

"That probably isn't enough explosive to kill him," Marty said, "You might injure his hand, or if it's in his pocket, maybe burn his leg, but—"

"Like I already told you, it'll be up around his ear at the exact moment," Carson assured him.

"And how do you know that?"

"Because I'm going to make the call," Carson said. "Not only that, I'm going to be sitting right across from him when it happens."

Marty gave him a confused look. "How…?"

Carson smiled wide. "I think it's time for me and Tanner Fritz to bury the hatchet, don't you? And what better way to smooth things out than over a nice dinner together?"

Chapter Thirty

Barry

Barry had been staring at the login screen for some time. He'd already typed in his username, Gladiator1968 and his password, which was jumbled mix of numbers, letters, and symbols that were so random even he'd struggled to commit them to memory.

When he'd mentioned the deep web to the group, he saw varying levels of understanding in their expressions. Complete ignorance from Carson, some comprehension from Marty, and clear understanding from Serena. When he said *dark* web, only Serena's expression remained unchanged.

Barry had resisted the siren's call of an online life after his accident. It was an alluring one. On the 'net, no one could hear his stutter, or see his ticks. His typing may have been slower than it once was, but that was the only tell when it came to betraying his true condition. Online, he could be whoever he wanted.

For a while, he was Gladiator1968.

For a man who lived most of his life in code, he had expected an online existence to hold more power, to seem more real to him, than it actually did. Maybe because he could see the man behind the curtain, like a filmmaker who went to the movies or a magician at a magic show, it lost its thrill for him. Online was online, real life was real life.

But the two realms co-existed, and despite his refusal to retreat into an online world, Barry still became versed in its ways. The one thing that was positively magical was that you could get anything if you knew where to look.

Anything.

It was magical, in a way. Instead of pixie dust, however, the magic came from anonymity. Multiple, redundant mechanisms maintained and assured mutual anonymity, and with identity stripped away, the possibilities were damn near limitless.

Barry hit the 'enter' key, and went down the rabbit hole.

An hour later, he found exactly what he was looking for. A cell phone that matched Tanner's model, wired for detonation. All Carson had to do was call from a specific number. Two full seconds after Tanner answered, it would explode. The seller even threw in a cheap burner phone and programmed with the trigger number.

Barry asked about the force of the explosion. He found it interesting that Marty's objection to the plan had merit. The seller couldn't guarantee fatality, especially if the phone wasn't near the recipient's head.

Hopefully Carson can manage that.

They dickered briefly over price. Barry begrudgingly fronted the money. Carson was good for it. Anyone who paid off when he lost at gambling like he did wouldn't welsh on something like this.

Welsh? Is that racist? Everything is these days.

Barry considered while the anonymous transfer went through. He knew his funds were bouncing from VPN to VPN, disguising their origin and destination.

The Welsh question made him angry at Siegelman again. His bullshit complaint had made Barry's situation worse. And even though Tanner had technically rescued him from termination, the banishment from the Chismo office burned in his gut. His initial gratitude had faded once he realized he wasn't being reassigned but was being put out to pasture, hung out on a limb Tanner would eventually sever. Over time, his services would be utilized less and less, if at all, and corporate would decide they couldn't justify the expense and fire him. It was only a matter of time. Tanner didn't save him. The man just didn't have the guts to actually fire him, and took the coward's way out.

He wished Lena were there. She would have seen the ruse for what it was right from the get-go. Together they could have come up with a way to counter it.

Lena.

Her sudden ghosting of him cut even deeper than Tanner's betrayal. Why would she come on so strong, going so far as to conspire *murder* with him, only to drop off into radio silence? It didn't make sense.

The computer dinged.

Transfer complete.

Barry waited for a few tense moments. Then a set of simple instructions appeared on the screen. He could pick up his purchase in two hours in a garbage can at a park.

He knew that park. It was only a couple of miles from Lena's house. Maybe he should stop by, force her to talk to him, and explain…

Explain what?

She'd made her point pretty clear, hadn't she? For whatever reason, she'd had enough of him.

Maybe it wasn't him, though. She hadn't been to work, either. It could be that she just picked up and left town for some reason. Was their attempted run-down on Tanner generating heat that he didn't know about? Were the police aware, and had they picked up Lena?

He didn't think so. But it was possible that her past had caught up to her and forced her to lay low for a while. He'd like to think that she'd reach out to him, maybe even ask him to go on the run with her. Then again, she had been very protective. He could see how she might not want to put him in danger.

Picking up his phone, he dialed Lena for what seemed like the thousandth time. It rang and rang before the carrier's message played. "This subscriber has a mailbox that is full." He slid to the floor and curled up in a fetal position, miserable and unable to understand why she didn't want to talk to him anymore.

"What d-d-did I-I do?" he asked. "W-w-what?"

Barry let out a long, dispirited moan. He didn't know the answer. All he knew for sure was that, as much as he wanted to see Tanner get what he had coming, there was no way he was going to go pick up Carson's goddamn death phone.

Someone else could do it.

Chapter Thirty-One

Serena

Carson's an idiot, an honest-to-God moron.

She was thinking about his harebrained plot as she walked to the subway.

But he has an idiot's luck.

She considered his plan while she waited with the throngs of commuters on their way home at the end of the workday—good thing too because the subway platform was hot as hell, an inferno of body heat and electrical transformer radiation. Concerning herself with Carson's idea distracted her from the discomfort.

Look at all these poor schmucks, she mused. They rode these cattle cars every day. She was standing among them only because her car was in the shop for service. Well, that and the fact that she wasn't going to drive her own car to go pick up a dark web explosive device that was going to be used in an idiot's murder plan.

A plan that might just work...

She took a shallow breath, catching a whiff of the many-layered scent of the platform. Perfume, body odor, oil, cologne, and the metallic tinge of charged electricity all drifted past her in varied strength. *How do people do this every day? Once, twice a year I can deal with this but more than that...? You've got to be out of your mind.*

She held the non-descript brown paper bag in her left hand. It had been right where Barry said it would be, at the top of a garbage can in the park, up against the inside of the can and covered by specific fast food bag. She had to admire the level of competent subterfuge on the part of whomever Barry dealt with to score the death phone.

Actually, Barry being adept at navigating the dark web was impressive, too. She'd drawn him into the conspiracy for his computer skills, but hadn't imagined they extended to this level of criminality. She'd should have known better, but Barry still had the capacity to surprise her.

The cloning program he gave her was more along the lines of what she'd expected him to contribute. It was simple enough and he promised it would be fast. Just a quick connection to a USB cable, sixty seconds to upload, another sixty to download, and then the program would self-delete. Given Barry's software prowess and his knowledge of Chismo's systems, she felt confident that there'd be no trace of the program left behind.

This might work, she thought again. *Carson's dumb ass plan might work.*

And then the direction of her thoughts did a one-eighty. *Why am I helping this jerk? Do I even care if this works or not? If it does, I don't get my shot at Tanner. And Carson's original plan was ridiculous. He probably dreamed it up watching a James Bond movie. A man-child who still thinks Bond works for the CIA doesn't have the mental wherewithal to pull it off on his own. Instead, he's got Barry and me doing his work for him. What an idiot I am.*

She was worked up. Coupled with the sweltering platform heat she began to sweat heavily. She pulled off her blazer and arched her back, not caring if she exposed some generous side boob in the process. A guy looked up from his iPad and nearly fell over trying to get a better view.

Look at this yokel. I took off my jacket and he almost fell on his face. How easy it would be to nudge him onto the tracks just as a train roared into the station.

Tickled by the scenario, she shook her head.

Easy to do.

Hard not to get caught.

Her thoughts turned back to the task at hand. Take the phone back to the office. Get hold of Tanner's phone, clone it onto the death phone, and replace it before he left the office for the day. Easy peasy.

She glanced at her own phone. It wasn't even one yet. Tanner wouldn't be back from his meeting at corporate until late in the day. She had plenty of time. Too much, actually.

She was still being ogled by the guy with the iPad. He was ruggedly good-looking and well built.

Time for a little diversion, she mused.

"Excuse me," she said in the most winsome voice possible. "I'm not familiar with the subway and I don't know where to… get off. Do you think you could help me?"

Chapter Thirty-Two

Carson

They buried the hatchet over drinks, or at least that's what Carson pretended to do. They both had an old fashioned, their choice in college when they were trying to affect the cultured but rugged persona. Carson hadn't had one since the day he heard about Santo Corp acquiring Chismo.

"I was surprised when you called," Tanner said. "It's been a while."

"*It's been a while,*" Carson sang in his nineties grunge voice.

Tanner laughed, but Carson sensed it was more out of nostalgia than true amusement. That didn't surprise him. Tanner had been putting on airs for a while. Carson's sophomoric, salesman style of humor was beneath him now.

"Seriously, though," Tanner said. "I was surprised."

"So was I," Carson told him. "I didn't plan it or anything."

"Then, what? You just woke up today and decided we needed to mend the fence?"

Carson took a sip of his drink. "Something like that." He glanced at his phone.

So close now.

Half an hour earlier, Serena had met him to drop off the burner-triggered phone just up the street from restaurant where he was to meet Tanner. She was strangely quiet during the exchange, but gave him a thumbs-up, so he knew the cell phone clone-and-swap had been successful. That meant his plan would work.

His plan was simple, like he told Marty a plan should be. At the time he'd chosen, he would excuse himself to go to the bathroom. As soon as he was out of Tanner's line of sight, he'd call the death phone from the burner. Tanner would answer the phone, and two seconds later, *bam!* That'd be all she wrote.

"Well, I'm glad you did," Tanner told him. "I've missed you, buddy."

I'm sure you have. But your piles of money probably softened the blow.

"I guess I missed you, too," Carson said. "That's why I called."

The waiter appeared at the table. "Will you gentlemen be ordering, or are you waiting for others to join you?"

"Just us," Tanner said, "but . . . I think we'll go another round first, then dinner." He glanced at Carson. "Yes?"

"Sounds good to me."

The waiter nodded primly and cruised away.

Tanner leaned in. "Listen, now that we're both here, let's clear the air, huh?"

Carson checked his watch surreptitiously. "Sure."

"You want to go first, or should I?"

"Doesn't matter."

Tanner considered. "Well, since you're the one who reached out, I'll talk first."

"Okay."

Tanner took a deep breath. Then his phone buzzed, interrupting whatever he'd been planning to say. He looked annoyed, but checked his message. After swiping at it a couple of times, he tapped it in frustration.

"Problem?" Carson asked.

Tanner frowned. "My phone's acting up, is all."

"I heard those models had issues. Freezing up, dropped calls, batteries exploding."

Tanner looked up. "Really?"

"Pretty sure. Weren't they banned from airplanes or something?"

Tanner's brow furrowed. "I read about that, but I didn't think…" He shrugged. "Oh, well. I'll have Serena check into it for me tomorrow."

Carson suppressed a grin, masking it with a sip of his old fashioned.

That won't be necessary, dick.

Tanner finished with his message and pushed the phone to the side. "Where were we?"

"Clearing the air. You were going first."

"That's right." Tanner leaned forward and stared at Carson meaningfully. "I want you to know that when I bought your share of the company I had no idea Santo Corp was going to acquire us."

Sure you didn't.

"In fact," Tanner continued, "they didn't even reach out until weeks later."

You mean you didn't close on the details until weeks later. Lying fuck.

"I'm sorry if you ever thought differently," Tanner said. "But that's the truth."

Bullshit.

"I believe you," Carson said.

Tanner smiled, seeming slightly relieved. "Good. I always thought that was why you were angry with me. That you thought I screwed you somehow."

"I didn't."

Tanner's expression turned dubious. "Well, after you left the company, I'd heard that was what you were saying."

"Who said that?"

"Several people."

"Several liars."

Tanner shrugged. "Either way, I can understand how you might feel. I just want you to know it wasn't true."

"All right."

Even if he knew Tanner wasn't lying through his perfectly whitened teeth, it didn't matter to Carson. Tanner still had the money and the company, and he had neither.

"Why were you mad, then?" Tanner asked.

"I wasn't."

"Carson, you left the company. *Our* company. You had to be at least a little bit angry."

"I couldn't stay," Carson explained. "I couldn't go from co-CEO to some salaried goof. Nobody would respect me. I had to leave."

Tanner considered. "Maybe. But it seemed like more than that."

Jesus, will you stop already?

"I was ashamed, okay?" Carson let a little of the

very real frustration and tension he was feeling seep into his tone. "I didn't want anyone to know about my run of bad luck, and I couldn't be just another guy working there after I was a top man. Get it?"

"I get it." Tanner was quiet for a few moments. Then he said, "You know, I'm sorry for what you thought happened with the acquisition, but I'm more sorry about something else."

"What?"

"When you came to me and told me about your gambling debts, I have to admit, I was angry with you. Your gambling problem put everything at risk."

"It's not a *problem*. I just had a run of bad luck, thanks to a couple of kickers who couldn't nail a goddamn extra point."

"It was a lot of money," Tanner said. "And if you remember, I paid out your shares above market value, too."

"I remember."

But you did okay, didn't you? Especially since you already had the Santo deal in your pocket.

"That lack of capital became an issue once Santo Corp expressed interest," Tanner continued. "I had to scramble to get things in order, and cut corners in place I probably shouldn't." His face darkened. "Just ask Barry."

Why the hell would I ask Barry about you ripping me off?

"But I don't know why I'm even talking about that. It wasn't the money that made me mad at you. It was that your needing the money from me took something important away from the company, and from me." He gave Carson an intense stare. "Chismo lost its best dealmaker, and I lost one of my best friends."

He was good, Carson had to admit. Tanner had honed his public image, and he was bringing his A-game tonight. If Carson didn't know better, he'd be tempted to believe what Tanner was saying.

For the sake of getting past all of this sanctimonious bullshit, he said, "Well, I still can't come back to work for you, but at least you can have your friend back."

"I'm glad." Tanner's smile was radiant. "That was the more important of the two, anyway."

Oh, my God. Pour a little syrup on the double chocolate cake, why don't you?

Carson raised his old fashioned. "Here's to that, then."

Tanner clinked his glass and they drank. As Carson lowered his glass, he checked the time.

Two minutes to go.

Wanting to move on past the schmaltz, Carson said, "Nice Lambo, by the way. But I wish you'd have let me fix you up with something less exotic, and more American."

"You still can. The Lamborghini isn't mine."

"What?"

"It's a charity thing," Tanner said.

Carson listened while Tanner explained how Chismo had purchased the car so that it could be raffled off for the children's cancer charity. "Tickets are five hundred bucks or five for two thousand," he said. "And the only way it isn't tax deductible is if you win the Lamborghini."

"Did Marty tell you that?"

Sadness tinged Tanner's features. "No, the in-house accountants did. I . . . I haven't seen Marty since . . . well, you know."

"Since Andrea."

"Yeah." Tanner sipped at his drink. "I feel bad about that, I really do but when I first saw her across the room . . ." He shook his head. "What can I say? It was love at first sight."

"But she was already married."

"I know."

"To your friend."

"I know." Tanner looked uncomfortable. "But Marty and I had drifted apart after college. I only saw him once in a while for business. I'd never met Andrea before that night."

"The night of the party for the Santo acquisition?"

"Yes, that was it."

So you screwed Marty and me over on the same night. Well done, ass-munch. If you'd somehow managed to push a wall of servers over onto Barry's head right before the party, you could have had the hat trick.

"You have to understand, Carson. She told me she was miserable in her marriage. She was going to divorce him no matter what."

R-i-i-ight.

"I didn't know that," he said, glancing at his watch.

"Marty probably didn't, either." Tanner stared into his drink. "Still, the timing wasn't great."

"No," Carson agreed.

Almost go time.

No Dibs On Murder

Tanner's phone rang.

Carson cringed.

God forbid he got tied up on a long call. It'd fuck up everything. He watched as Tanner stared at the caller ID.

A moment passed and Tanner let the call go to Voicemail. He stowed the phone in his pocket. "Fucking sharks," he swore.

"Trouble?" Carson asked.

"Just BS. I was out to dinner with my boss and—"

Carson's jaw dropped. "Wait . . . you have a boss?"

"Come on, Carson—everyone's got a boss. Thirty-two year old Japanese gal—Executive VP over all Santo's subsidiaries."

"How'd she climb the ladder so fast?" he asked, hoping for tawdry details.

"She's as sharp as a tack—London School of Economics, smart, diligent..." He gulped his drink. "Not hard on the eyes, either."

"Yeah?" Carson asked, his voice drifting toward lurid.

Tanner chuckled and shook his head. "It's not like that, trust me."

Shit—he wasn't cheating on Andrea? That really sucked. Carson whet his whistle. "And she's busting your balls?" *Good, I hope she crucifies his ass.*

"Yes, but not the way you'd think. We'd just had our regular dinner meeting and were walking to the car when some jalopy comes flying by and cleaves a Johnny pump right off the sidewalk—craziest thing I ever saw. A blast of water shot out and lifted this ninety-five pound girl up in the air. She smashed down and ruptured both her implants."

Carson choked on his cocktail.

"She's suing me over it."

"Suing you? Over what?"

"Medical bills. Pain. Suffering. *Embarrassment.*" He shook his head. "The whole thing is eating a hole in my stomach, if you want the truth. That was her lawyer on the phone—third time he's called today, but fuck 'em. Who's he to interrupt us?"

He raised his glass. They toasted. "Life is short," Tanner said. "Everyone deserves to be happy."

Carson resisted the urge to laugh. He expected to be very happy, very shortly.

Tanner looked up from his drink. "Same with the kids the charity works with. They deserve to be happy, despite what they're dealing with. That's why I support them so much. That, and my little brother, I suppose."

Carson stole a last look at his watch. Ninety seconds to go. He decided to leave for the restroom now. If Tanner started in about losing his kid brother to cancer, he'd be trapped at the table. He knew it didn't actually matter when he made the call to the death phone, but he had a plan and wanted to stick to it.

"He was only seven," Tanner began.

"I've gotta go to the bathroom," Carson said, standing up. "Hold that thought."

"Wait up," Tanner said. He took a final swig of his drink. "I'll join you, and then we'll order a couple of steaks, huh?"

Carson hesitated. He hadn't counted on this. He

considered his options, and realized there was only one.

"Sure."

They headed to the bathroom. Carson considered the curve ball in his plan and how to deal with it.

"Wow, you're in a hurry," Tanner observed.

"I really gotta go," Carson said as they walked past an older couple. The man at the table scowled at him and his date curled her lip in disgust.

Carson ignored them. Once in the bathroom, he took the first open stall. He removed his burner phone and sat down on the lid of the toilet seat, staring down at it.

He wanted to see that moment when his revenge landed on Tanner like a ton of bricks. He supposed he could wait a while, head back to the table for steaks, and find another reason to step away later. But a gnawing sense of potential failure was growing in his stomach. His instincts said that if he didn't do it soon, he'd miss his chance.

The door of the stall next to him opened and closed. He heard the jingle of a belt buckle and the rustle of slacks as the man sat down. A moment later, there came a juicy fart.

Carson flipped open the burner phone. Tanner's number was already set to speed dial. Should he do it now?

The unmistakable sound of diarrhea came from the stall next to him. Then the man grunted, and the sound of his voice broke through Carson's worried thoughts.

Tanner?

Was that Tanner next to him?

Carson dipped his head and tried to look under the stall. He couldn't recognize the shoes, but the slacks pooled around the man's ankles looked like they could be Tanner's.

Carefully, Carson stood. Pressing a hand against the opposite wall, he stepped up onto the toilet. When he'd managed that without any noise he brought his other leg up behind him. Another grunt gave him the cover he needed. He sprang forward, pushing off on his rear foot.

Standing precariously on the toilet lid, and holding the burner phone in one hand, Carson leaned over the top of the stall and peeked down.

Sure enough, it was Tanner-Goddamn-Fritz, sitting on the porcelain throne, having a very nervous, watery shit. Carson wondered at the fact that Mister Together was stressed about their meeting. Then he thought that maybe it was the lawsuit he'd mentioned earlier. *Or too much hooch on an empty stomach.*

Not that it mattered.

Carson knew this wasn't perfect but his intuition told him the time was right. He pressed the speed dial.

A moment later, Tanner's phone buzzed. Tanner leaned forward and dug into his pants pocket. He held up the phone and peered at the screen.

Answer it, Carson thought. *Come on!*

Tanner seemed to consider doing just that. Then he reached up with his finger and swiped upward.

Tanner raised the phone toward his ear, but it slipped from his fingers. Carson watched over the top of the stall in shock as Tanner grasped at it, knocking it up in the air slightly. His ex-friend grasped and fumbled at the phone as if he were playing hot potato with it. The phone slipped through his fingers and fell straight downward, between his open legs and into the toilet.

"Oh, shit!" Tanner cried.

He stood and reached for the toilet paper.

Oh, shit is right, Carson thought.

The explosion happened a second later. Liquid flew upward from the toilet, covering the inside of the stall. A powerful blast of the revolting substance struck Carson full in the face as he stared downward, coating him like a mud mask.

Chapter Thirty-Three

Barry

Where have my balls gone? Barry thought as he walked away from Lena's place.

He'd staked out her rental home for most of an hour hoping to see movement inside or better still, catch her coming or going, a chance to confront her face to face and gather the bitter truth.

"It's over," he imagined her saying. "I'm done. I thought you had guts but now I know that's what I wanted to see. You're a loser, Barry . . . a fucking loser. Take a walk."

He'd fought with himself for the strength to knock on the door but his courage was lacking. He finally left with his shoulders arched forward and the brunt of his fears slicing through him like a jagged razor.

He was the last one to arrive at Carson's place. The others were sitting around in silence. No one complained about his tardiness. "I guess I-I haven't missed much?" He looked to the others for a response.

"I suggested we hold the meeting in the can," Marty said with a snicker, "because Carson's brilliant plan went to shit."

"Yeah, fuck you, Stitch. At least my plan wasn't a goddamn peanut butter bomb."

"It still didn't work."

Carson didn't reply.

Marty didn't relent. "How'd you keep from getting caught? I mean, you said your face was covered with—"

"I know what I said." Carson frowned, then sighed. "Tanner was yelling in pain. The back of his legs took a beating. I ran into the stall to help him. By the time I pulled him out of there and pretended to make sure he was okay, it made sense that I was a mess, too. Besides, he wasn't paying much attention at the time. He was just cursing out his phone."

"So now he's suspicious," Serena stated.

"No," Carson said. "That's the thing. I made some offhand remark about the battery, and he seized on that. He blames the manufacturer."

"So you two are pals again?"

Carson nodded glumly.

Barry grunted. He knew that wasn't the outcome Carson was hoping for. As much as he looked forward to Tanner getting what he deserved, it didn't break his heart to see Carson looking defeated.

"Look at this way," Marty said. "You saved two hundred buck on a spa day, but still got a shit facial. You didn't even have to deal with cucumber slices."

"Shut up."

"But you hate cucumbers."

"Oh zip it, both of you!" Serena barked. "I am so sick and tired of you whining like wet cats. At least Barry had the balls to suffer in silence. You don't see him crying in his beer like the two of you. He tried, he failed, and he's over it. Now it's time for you two to get over it as well."

Barry smiled on the inside. He would have preferred Lena's fierce advocacy, but if she was gone, it didn't hurt to have Serena in his corner again.

"Yeah," Carson said sarcastically, "Barry's hit and run attempt with Granny Clampett was a real masterstroke."

"F-f-fuck you, Carson. At least I didn't take a b-b-bucket of shit in the face."

Serena chimed in. "That's right Carson, and . . ."

"And *what*?" Carson snapped.

"Just for the record, Barry's a hell of a lot better in bed than you are."

"The hell."

"He's hung like a horse, too."

Carson gave her a dubious stare.

She cocked her head at him. "What, all those years in the university locker room you never caught a glimpse of the python?"

Oh! *Oh that's good*! That she was exaggerating a little didn't matter. She was putting Carson in his place, and that felt good. He blew Serena a kiss.

"That's bullshit," Carson said, shaking his head.

"It's true shit," Serena said, grinning. "Your specialty."

Carson snapped off a middle finger. "And *I'm* the child in the group?"

"Not a child," Serena cooed, "Just the one with the infant dick."

"Fuck you, Serena. You never complained."

"Nothing wrong with a tight va-jay-jay, Carson.

A needle dick on the other hand . . ."

Barry let out a chuckle. He noticed Marty smiling, too.

Carson flipped two independent birds and stalked off to the kitchen. He popped the cap and began swigging beer with his back turned to them.

"L-l-lighten up," Barry said.

"Yeah, fuck you, Barry."

"What's the matter? Can't take it? You give it pretty good."

Carson finished chugging the beer, then reached into the fridge for another.

Serena watched the exchange, an amused look on her face. Then she said, "You three stooges had your chance. It's time to step aside."

Carson wheeled around. "What's your fucking stake in this anyway, Serena? What's Tanner ever done to you?"

"None of you fucking business. I said I'm in and I'm in. That's all you need to know."

"Now hold on," Marty said. "*I'd* like to know too. I mean we're trying to kill someone. Where's your hate coming from?"

"It's coming from right here," she said, flipping him a middle finger.

Marty shook his head. "Not good enough."

"Maybe I was bored," Serena snapped. "Is that all right?"

"You were bored?" Marty asked. "That's it? You were bored so you decided you'd throw in on a murder conspiracy?"

"Yes. I was bored and it sounded like two tons of fun. I got to listen in while you three bobbleheads did your cock fighting and boasted about how clever you were. Most fun I've ever had."

"Seriously?"

"Yes, Marty—seriously."

Carson shook his head. "I don't believe it—not for one-fucking-minute. You were bored? I call bullshit."

"It was good enough for Ally Sheedy, wasn't it?"

"Who?" Carson asked.

"Ally Sheedy," she said. "What, you never watched *The Breakfast Club*?

Carson rolled his eyes.

"No way," Marty said

"What can I tell you? I got tired of antiquing. This seemed like fun."

Barry wanted to know her motive as well but he wasn't going to team up with Carson and Marty against his one ally. Then idea crossed his mind. He knew she'd be savvy enough to play along. "T-t-tell them," he said. "What's the harm?" He could see the workings of her mind. It took a nanosecond for her to join him on the same page.

"I'm not going to waste my breath," she said. "I don't need these two school boys to know my business."

"It-it'll get them off your b-b-back. If you want, I-I…"

"Yeah, all right. Fine." She put up her hand shielding her face. "Just get it over with."

"What's the story, Barry?" Marty asked.

Barry looked to her for approval. She nodded. "The ac-acquisition deal—Serena bro-bro-brokered it. Tanner shafted her on her commission. That's w-why she wants him d-dead. She was d-d-due one point on the deal."

"WHAT?" Carson howled. "Serena, is this true?"

"You bet your bullshit, Carson. Santo paid Tanner thirty-one mil and I got screwed out of three hundred grand. I didn't even get a promotion out of the deal. So ask me again why I want the sonofabitch dead." She angled her head so that only Barry could see her face and winked at him.

Wow! That's one impressive line of bullshit. She really took the ball and ran with it, Barry thought. *Least I could do for her after she called Carson a needle dick.*

"It doesn't make sense," Carson said doubtfully. "How's the head of HR broker a deal like this?"

"By knowing the head of HR for Santo Corp, who is sleeping with the CEO," Serena snapped back. "Fat white men with cigars aren't the only people who can make back room deals, Carson."

Carson glowered, but seemed to accept her explanation. "One thing I've got to know," he said. "Did the deal come about before or after Tanner bought my equity?"

"You mean before Tanner bailed your ass out? After, Carson. Well after. In fact, your payout drained the company so badly it forced Tanner to look for a white knight. I brokered the deal with Santo and the rest is history, you ungrateful sack of shit. So stop bellyaching about how he screwed you out of your equity when what he really did was save your gambling-debt ass."

Barry watched on in wonder. Carson hadn't been on the receiving end of a good ass-kicking in as long as he could remember. *Hell, he certainly doesn't deserve sympathy. He's always been a tool and since getting the heave-ho from Chismo...* well, he'd become a merciless prick, a guy who got off on the misery of others. For the first time in a long time, and in spite of his worry about Lena, Barry was enjoying every moment of it.

Chapter Thirty-Four

Serena

Serena watched Ricardo push the vacuum down the corridor of the executive office wing, then checked her watch. "The man's like a machine," she murmured within the confines of her glass-walled office.

Seven thirty-eight—he'll be done in seven minutes flat, then off to the next building in the complex.

She'd always been kind to Ricardo, as she was to most hardworking types. He cleaned the Chismo offices three times a week, arriving promptly at five-fifteen every Monday, Wednesday, and Friday.

"*Hola*, Ricardo," she said as she stood and walked to the doorway. She was dressed to the nines in a form-fitting gown and pumps. She was certain he'd notice her despite the loud roar of the vacuum. She wasn't wrong. He switched off the vacuum and waved in a timid manner.

Poor SOB. He's always afraid of getting fired, she thought as she handed him a small gift box emblazoned with the Chismo logo. "A little something for your daughter—the teenager. She loves music, right?"

"*Música, si.*" He seemed very unsure of himself and apprehensive about accepting a gift.

"It's a Bluetooth speaker. You know, *Bluetooth*?"

He said he understood but the truth was he didn't. He tapped a capped tooth. "*Si*, blue *Azul*."

She smiled warmly. "Never mind. Give it to Rosa. She'll know what to do with it."

He nodded appreciatively, thanking her for the generous gift but still looking uneasy. "It's okay to take?"

"Absolutely."

"Thanks you so much."

"I have to replace your security tag, Ricardo." Without waiting she unclipped the tag from his shirt pocket and replaced it with a new one. "Security update. Thanks for all your good work. I won't keep you—I know you've got three more buildings to clean before you head home." She pocketed his old tag.

"*Si, tres mas. Gracias, Senorita* Serena. Appreciate. *Gracias.*"

Atta boy, Ricardo. He'd be past the security turnstile in a few minutes after scanning the new tag, which like the original, read Majestic Cleaning Company. But the new tag had been encoded with Serena's security code, so when he left, the security system would record it as Serena and not Ricardo who'd gone home for the night.

She recognized the familiar silence of the office after Ricardo had completed his work and left for the evening. She was alone in the Chismo office suite. Checking her watch again, she slipped off her pumps and gown and donned black coveralls and kicks. She snatched a rectangular tote bag and hurried to the staircase. Taking the stairs two and three at a time

No Dibs On Murder

she was on the building roof in no time flat, setting up her sniper nest.

She leveled the rifle and began checking the ballistic settings. She'd estimated the distance by pacing it off earlier in the day, and it was no further than what she practiced for on the range. The wind direction and speed worried her, though. It was an unusually windy day with gusts kicking up randomly. She knew it would affect the bullet's trajectory but couldn't be sure by how much.

Tanner's parking spot was only three hundred feet away. She planned to pick him off when he arrived to raffle off the Lamborghini. Arriving before the crowd, he'd be more or less alone in the parking lot. The event had been staged outdoors at the far end of the Chismo building on the company campus.

One trigger pull. One shot.

She'd be back in her office before anyone arrived at the scene.

That is if anyone reacts to the solitary shot, she mused, somewhat confident that no one would respond to the quick crack of the rifle.

She tried to guess how to adjust for the wind speed, but it was impossible due to the intermittent gusts. "This sucks!" she said and squeezed her eye to the scope just as Tanner's white Range Rover pulled into the lot. The appearance of the white SUV gave her a moment's pause. She'd forgotten that the screaming yellow Lamborghini had been professionally detailed and was already at the venue, ready for the presentation.

The Range Rover slid into the spot. Serena was ready, her sights trained on where he would stand when he pushed the door closed. *One Shot.* One clean shot before breaking down the rifle and racing back to her office.

She could see him through the windshield getting ready. He popped a mint into his mouth, before stashing his new cellphone in his jacket pocket, and checking his hair in the vanity mirror.

"Come and get it, you vain motherfucker."

She saw the driver's door open and a hand sewn moccasin step out of the car.

"This is it," she whispered.

Still your breath. Relax. She began the gentle pullback on the trigger. *Come on, you bastard. Get out of the car.*

Tanner put his hand on the doorsill and boosted himself out of the SUV.

She slowly moved the crosshairs until they were right between his eyes.

Slowly back on the trigger.

Slowly.

Slowly.

Crack!

A gust whipped by just as the round exploded from the barrel, moving a tree branch directly in the path of the bullet, deflecting it.

Tanner jumped as a tree branch came crashing down on the hood of the Range Rover. "Son of a bitch," he swore loudly, completely oblivious to the .338 Lapua Magnum bullet that had severed the branch and gone on to imbed itself in a berm that anchored a row of giant arborvitae. The hood was badly creased and the windshield shattered. He shook his head, seemed to sigh deeply, and walked away.

"Fuck!" Serena tucked the rifle under her arm and hightailed it off the roof.

She'd missed her chance.

Serena stowed the rifle in the bottom drawer of the wide file cabinet in her office and locked it. She'd smuggle the weapon out later, but now she needed to make an appearance at the raffle. She quickly changed back into her gown and pumps before stuffing the coveralls and kicks in a garbage bag she'd toss in the utility room trash after passing through the security plaza with Ricardo's tag. While there, she'd have to switch the ID tags back, too. That was no problem, though. Ricardo always left his tag on the cart when he left after completing the cleaning service.

"Son of a bitch. Son of a fucking *bitch*." She was furious as she got into the elevator and even hotter as she scanned Ricardo's tag at the security plaza. *All for nothing. The planning. The details. Shit. Tanner's still alive. I didn't even scare the SOB.* Yes, the sudden falling branch startled him but as far as the bullet meant to take his life...

He didn't have a clue, not a fucking clue. It was as if it didn't happen.

By the time she reached the campus, the seats were eighty percent full and Tanner looked completely over the falling branch mishap. He was once again his unflappable self, every hair in place, smile glowing.

She sat silently as the seats around her filled. The

outer reaches of the campus were crowded as well, standing room only. She was practically oblivious as Tanner addressed the audience, boasting about the nearly twenty-five hundred tickets that had been sold and the one million plus that had been raised for the local Children's Cancer Foundation.

The evening had a surreal quality. The strong winds had subsided just in time for Tanner to take center stage. It was if even the weather bowed to his will. The crowd buzzed continuously as the clock ticked down to the winner announcement. Serena was there but wasn't. Time was transpiring but she was frozen in the moment, allowing disappointment to eat away at her.

Who would win the exotic sports car?

Who cared?

Who had lost, though? Serena thought. *Me. I did. I can't fucking believe it.*

She hardly noticed as a beautiful little bald child was rolled out in a wheelchair and picked the winning ticket from the raffle drum. Only an occasional word broke through her trance.

"And the winner is . . ."

She shook her head in disbelief as the winner walked onto the stage amidst a blizzard of cheers. His name was Dante Mabuhay, a fifty-six year old Filipino school bus driver wearing baggy pants and sandals. His greasy black hair was encrusted with dandruff flakes the size of snowballs.

"Ever driven a Lambo?" Tanner said as he interviewed the bus driver who had purchased a solitary ticket in memory of his deceased nephew.

"What kind of question is that?" Serena

grumbled. "Only when his Rolls Royce is in the shop. *You douchebag!*"

"Are you kidding?" Mabuhay said. "I drive a Chrysler minivan."

"Well, here are the keys." Tanner said handing them over. "Take it easy until you get used to her, sport. She's a real beast."

Mabuhay's eyes were as large as hardboiled eggs as the scissor door opened and he got in. He placed his foot on the brake and hit the starter button. The 5.2-liter V-10 came to life with the fury of 630 horses. He revved the engine, lightly at first and then more heavily as he responded to the crowd's enthusiasm, pushing harder, burying the gas pedal. The roar of the engine built to an ear-shattering scream.

"We should've given away a set of earplugs with every ticket purchased," Tanner quipped, his amplified voice just barely audible above the sound of ten thundering cylinders. An exhibition course had been set up with cones just beyond the campus. "Okay, sport," he said gesturing to the coned course. "Take your victory lap."

Even from where she sat, it was clear to Serena that Mabuhay was drunk on the excitement. All the attention must have been like an intoxicant to a worker bee who went through life mostly invisible.

"Put her into gear!" Tanner encouraged him.

Mabuhay did what he was told.

The super-soft tires bit into the asphalt as the tachometer shot past six thousand RPM. Tanner was quick on his feet but not quick enough to avoid the charging bull. It gored him and threw him into the air, not to land until he crunched down on the asphalt some twenty-feet away.

Screams from the crowd masked the sound of the impact but it was clear how bad a hit Tanner had taken. Andrea ran toward him screaming and dozens nearby ran to his aid. A woman covered her mouth in horror and her young daughter vomited.

Serena watched the whole scene in amazement. She had been so high and mighty, mocking the other henchmen, picking apart their attempts, and belittling them privately. She wouldn't fail. Couldn't fail. She meticulously practiced her shot and had thought out her plan carefully—down to the smallest detail. She shook her head in disbelief. She'd fallen from her perch and for one heart-breaking moment realized that her failure put her on the same pitiful plane as the others.

Fate had outdone them all.

She was still in her seat as her cheekbones rose. The precarious nature of life had settled over her.

Life can be a son of a bitch, can't it, Tanner?

Tanner the evil wizard managed to get away with stealing Barry's head, Marty's heart, and Carson's confidence, as well as avoiding both her seduction and her wrath... only to get run over by a lottery Lamborghini driven by a Filipino bus driver.

She stood up and headed in the opposite direction, away from everyone else, recalling something her aunt used to say.

Man plans and God laughs.

Chapter Thirty-Five

Marty

He'd sat through most of the presentation alternating between feeling glum and anticipating Serena's big move. When the event labored on and nothing happened, he figured she'd missed her chance somehow and he ditched the anticipation and settled full time on glum, which was easy enough. All he had to do was watch Tanner work the crowd, a microphone in his hand. Everyone loved him, and responded to him.

Especially Andrea.

What a prick.

When Tanner finally announced the unlikely winner of the Lamborghini, Marty was glad. That meant the show was almost over, and he could slip out unnoticed. He didn't have the stomach to spend another minute witnessing the universal adulation of Tanner Fritz.

He held out a last, crazy hope that Serena's plan had involved a car bomb—why not, the woman was full of surprises these days—but when the lucky winner cranked the ignition, all he heard was the Lamborghini's engine rumbling to life. The crowd cheered and the new owner revved the engine.

"Enough of this," Marty muttered, and he stood

to leave.

Then something wonderful happened.

He heard the engine rev, the tires bite and squeal. And then the magnificent yellow sports car surged forward, directly toward Tanner Fritz.

Marty stared in awe. As if in slow motion, the front of the Lamborghini struck Tanner, scooping him up and hurling him high like a charging bull. Tanner seemed to hang in the air for a moment, then landed in a heap on the concrete nearby.

Pandemonium followed.

Marty stood stock-still as the world seemed to explode around him. Screams. People rushing past him and toward Tanner. The Lamborghini, fishtailing wildly before lurching to a stop. The slow-handed bus driver aghast by what he'd done.

Throngs of people bunched around Tanner. Calls for a doctor went out, and a man and a woman both immediately stepped forward, identifying themselves as physicians and volunteering their services.

"Call an ambulance!" someone shrieked.

"Call the police!" someone else demanded.

The raffle winner stood in the open doorway of his prize, gaping at the carnage he'd created. "No… I… I… it was just too powerful. It got away from me."

"Murderer!" cried someone in the crowd.

"I drive a mini-van," the man pleaded.

Marty took it all in. He didn't know how Serena had managed it, or if she'd actually had nothing to do with it at all. Maybe karma had taken a hand and called dibs on this one. He didn't care. Finally, *finally*, Tanner Fritz got what he had coming to him.

He spotted Andrea on the fringes of the crowd surrounding Tanner. She held her own arms tightly, as if shrinking from the sight. No one comforted her.

Marty was moving before he had time to think. This was what he'd waited for, and he needed to strike while iron was hot.

He brushed past several onlookers to reach Andrea's side. Tentatively, he snaked his arm around her, intending to pull her close to him. In his imagination, he saw her dissolving into tears. She'd turn to him, wrap her arms around him, and weep into his shoulder. He'd be the strength she needed, her rock, her newfound—

Andrea jumped as soon his fingers touched her upper arm. Turning, she saw him. Tears streaked her face, but another emotion clawed its way into her expression. Anger. "Marty! What the hell are you doing?"

"I thought you might need comfort," he said lamely.

"My husband just got hit by a car. Fuck off!"

She shoved him with both palms into his chest, turned away and ran to Tanner's side.

Marty stumbled back from the force of her push. He watched Andrea kneel beside her unconscious husband. The grief and worry on her face was visceral, and it cut through his heart like a scalpel.

He wanted to leave. He wanted to cry. He wanted to scream at everyone that Tanner got his and karma might be a bitch, but she's a fair one. He tried to take some dark joy in the scene, but he couldn't. All he could do was stare as the two off-duty doctors tended to Tanner, Andrea wept and held his hand,

and everyone else looked on in heartfelt shock.

Carson appeared at his side.

"Already got the stop sign from the widow, huh? Nice work, Stitch."

Chapter Thirty-Six

Carson

"Already got the stop sign from the widow, huh?" He grinned at Marty. "Nice work, Stitch."

Marty stared at him vacantly for a few seconds, then looked away.

"Christ," Carson muttered. "You're no fun."

He couldn't understand why Marty's biggest problem wasn't finding a way to resist jumping for joy and whooping to high heaven. That's what *he* felt like doing, and not doing it was a challenge.

Of course, it was the Andrea thing that had Marty in a funk. He'd made his move way too soon, and now he'd blown it. Poor Marty. He never did understand chicks.

Speaking of chicks, Carson had no clue how Serena managed to pull this one off, but he was impressed. She was one surprise after another, and this one topped them all. He glanced around the crowd, trying to find her, but she was nowhere to be seen.

Carson turned back to the main attraction. He watched in silence as a man in a bloody tuxedo shirt and woman in a little black dress tended to Tanner's injuries. Carson was no expert, but he could see blood coming from a head wound, and one of

Tanner's arms sat at an unnatural angle. He looked a little closer, and noticed that one of Tanner's legs was oddly bent as well.

Dude is seriously fucked up, he thought. *Couldn't happen to a nicer guy.*

Sirens erupted in the distance, drawing closer at startling speed. Then Carson remembered that First Memorial Hospital was less than a mile away. He supposed that was lucky.

But was it lucky enough? Or was this it for Tanner Fritz?

Carson's gaze swept over Tanner's limp body again. *I'd say it's three-to-one he's got internal injuries, and it is game over. Five-to-one he never wakes up and stays in a coma for years.*

Tanner's eyes flew open, and he let out a screech of pain.

Carson shrugged. Five-to-one were shit odds, anyway.

Tanner opened his eyes momentarily. He looked around frantically and saw Andrea clutching his hand. He smiled bravely at her, but Carson could see defeat in the man's eyes. Tanner tore his eyes away from Andrea. His gaze swept the crowd and he spotted Carson.

"Carson!" he croaked weakly.

Carson jumped slightly. Was an accusation coming? He almost yelled back, "It wasn't me, it was Serena!" but managed to keep his cool.

The sirens drew closer.

Tanner mouthed something, but Carson couldn't hear him.

"What?" he asked, not moving.

Tanner repeated himself.

"What?" Carson asked again.

"He wants you to come here," Andrea shouted.

"Me?"

Tanner managed a weak nod.

Carson stepped forward, and the crowd parted for him. For Tanner, he realized. *They parted for Tanner.* Either way, he quickly walked to the injured man's side, kneeling next to him. A hundred yards away, a screaming ambulance pulled into the parking lot and cut its siren. He heard doors open and close immediately.

"What is it?" Carson asked. Then he forced himself to add, "Buddy?"

"Come . . . with me," Tanner whispered. "To the hospital."

"Okay." Carson didn't know what else to say. How would it look if he refused?

The medics arrived at the throng and hollered for everyone to step back. They conferred with the doctors on scene and performed some quick triage. Then Tanner was loaded onto a gurney and hustled toward the ambulance. Andrea and Carson trotted alongside. The medics quickly loaded him inside the ambulance.

"Only one of you can ride in back with us," the medic informed them.

"No," Tanner said, his voice wavering. "Both."

The medic frowned. "No time to argue." He pointed to Andrea. "You're in back with me." Then, to Carson, "You ride up front."

The ride to the hospital was surreal. Lights. Sirens. Traffic parting way before them. Then the controlled chaos of the emergency room as the ER doctors resumed triage. Seemingly moments later, Tanner was wheeled away to surgery.

Carson sat in the waiting room next to Andrea. He didn't say anything. At first, she cried quietly, her head lowered into her palms. But after a while, she leaned over onto Carson's shoulder. He didn't move. He could tell that was all she wanted and he didn't mind.

He expected this to feel different. When he'd imagined getting revenge on Tanner, it always ended like one of the old Rocky movies. Well, the ones when Rocky *won*, not the first one, which Carson didn't like. He didn't celebrate losers.

But here he was. He'd won, or at least it seemed so. Even if it was Serena who did the heavy lifting, he'd gotten his revenge. So why was there no uplifting music or a feeling of elation? He didn't feel any of that. He didn't feel bad, either. He just felt . . . nothing.

After what seemed like hours, he realized Andrea had stopped leaning on him. Then he heard her yelling. That's when he saw that Marty had arrived. He stood in front of Andrea, shrinking away from her screams.

"Why are you even here? You were never there for me in our marriage but *now* you're here?"

Carson rose to restrain her but she kept shouting.

"Why? To gloat? To fucking *gloat*, Marty?"

"No, I . . ."

"Oh, go back to work, you son of a bitch. Or watch *Star Wars*. That's all you ever cared about."

"An—"

"Leave me alone!"

Carson was pretty certain this would have gone on for hours, but at that moment, a doctor appeared in the waiting area.

"Are you the family of Tanner Fritz?" he asked.

Andrea stepped forward quickly. "I'm his wife. Is he all right?"

"He's stable," the doctor said. "He's going to survive his injuries."

And just like that, all of Carson's previous feelings came rushing back in. *Of course* Tanner was going to survive getting run down by a Lamborghini. He was Tanner-Goddamn-Fritz.

The doctor quickly summarized Tanner's injuries for her—a broken arm, leg, and pelvis, along with some internal bleeding.

So I was right about that, Carson thought. *Ka-ching.*

"Can I see him?" Andrea asked.

"He's coming out of anesthesia, so yes. Come with me."

The doctor led her away.

Carson glanced over at Marty. Marty looked back at him.

"I guess he's gonna make it," Carson said.

"Looks that way."

They were quiet for a moment. Then Carson asked, "What are you doing here?"

"I thought. . ."

"Give it up, Stitch. Tanner or no Tanner, the girl is gone for you."

Marty hung his head, and Carson almost felt sorry for him.

"I should go," Marty said.

Marty looked at him expectantly, waiting. Carson didn't argue. He didn't say anything. He just looked back. After about thirty seconds, Marty sighed and trudged from the waiting area.

Carson thought about leaving, too, but worried about how it might look after Tanner's request to accompany him in the ambulance. He decided to get a cup of coffee from the nearby vending machine. If no one noticed him by the time he'd finished drinking it, he'd leave.

The Styrofoam cup was still half full when Andrea returned to the waiting area.

"He's asking for you," she said.

"*Me?*"

She shrugged. "Ever since he went to dinner with you . . . he can't stop talking about how you helped him after his phone malfunctioned and exploded, like you're his hero or something."

"Is that true?" Carson felt his guts churning, guilt choking him. "O-okay he said. If he wants me…"

The room was quiet. The light beep of machines were the only counterpoint to the silence. Carson tried to close the door gently, but the click sounded like a cannon shot.

Tanner's eyes flickered open. He saw Carson and waved him over, fluttering his fingers without raising his hand. Carson complied, standing awkwardly at the bedside.

"Sit," Tanner whispered hoarsely.

Carson found a chair and pulled it over. He sat

next to Tanner. "What is it?"

Tanner motioned toward a water cup with a straw in it. Carson picked it up and held it for him while Tanner sucked in some water, then he put it back on the table.

"I have to tell you something," Tanner said, his voice ragged. "Two things, really."

"I'm here," Carson said.

He couldn't know, could he?

Carson didn't think so. If he did, why would he ask for Carson? He wouldn't. He'd ask for Andrea and tell her to call the cops. That wouldn't be hard. They were probably all over the scene of the collision, and Carson was pretty sure he'd seen several of them here at the hospital.

No, that wasn't it.

"I'm glad . . ." Tanner began, "I'm glad we fixed things. Between us."

Carson forced himself to grin, bringing all of his salesman persona to bear. "We did kind of a shitty job of it."

Tanner smiled ever so slightly, but then it was gone again. "No, I'm serious. It means a lot to me." He motioned for Carson to lean closer.

"I have to tell you something else," Tanner said.

Carson forced a smile he didn't feel. "Yeah, buddy?"

Tanner told him, and in a night full of surprises, one after the other, he was goddamned if this wasn't the biggest surprise of them all.

Chapter Thirty-Seven

Serena

She'd dressed up as a naughty nurse for Halloween and costume parties over the years and knew her way around a nurse's cap and a white thigh-length nurse's dress over stockings and garters.

There's always activity in a hospital intensive care unit no matter the time of day but the corridor was somewhat quiet as Serena ducked into the ladies' room. She caught a glimpse of herself in the mirror and wrinkled her nose.

"Scrubs. *Yuck*. Stiff, boxy scrubs. I hardly look fetching in *this* clown suit." She shrugged. "Everyone's gender-boring these days, male and female hospital staff dressing as if they're on the assembly line in a sterile microchip factory. Blah."

The neutral attire did, however, make the task easier for her. Back in the day hospital staff wore uniforms specifically designed for each particular hospital, a uniform she would've had to steal in order to blend in. "I guess dull has its merits." She slid a hypodermic syringe out of her pocket and checked to make sure none of the epinephrine had leaked out. The cap was still on the needle and the medication remained intact. It was a large syringe with a three-inch plunger. She stowed it back in her pocket and opened the restroom door.

She lingered just inside the restroom doorway, her presence cloaked from staff walking by in the corridor. She didn't know how many staff members were on duty but took her time growing familiar with ebb and flow of the hallway traffic, developing a sense of how long it remained quiet.

She stepped from the restroom at exactly the wrong moment. Two physicians came around a corner, surprising her. She concealed her nervousness well. *Two overworked residents probably working seventy-two hours straight. Too tired to care who I am,* she thought. Her head down, she made her way around the floor peeking into rooms until she found Tanner's.

She admired Tanner as he lay sleeping in the darkened private room. The bruises and contusions only made him look more rugged, more handsome. It was as if a Hollywood makeup artist had purposely applied fake blood and prosthetics to garner more sympathy for the arresting fallen hero.

She'd never slept with Carson. He'd been her Mount Everest, but had always seemed impervious to her manipulations. Now, in a few minutes she'd have to cross him off her bucket list forever.

Well, off one of my bucket lists anyway, she mused. *Off one, onto another. God gives with one hand and takes with the other.*

As she watched him sleep an idea tickled her in an unusual way. She gave him a delicate kiss on the cheek and snapped a selfie of her in the act. She knew it was a little psycho, but she couldn't resist the memento.

He didn't move.

Go for more? She deliberated. *I am going to kill him, after all. What else will he sleep through?* First things first, though. She popped the cap off the needle and inserted it into Tanner's IV.

Okay, now where was I? She lifted his sheet and lowered her head to peek under it. "Should I or shouldn't I?" she said with a chuckle.

Her cellphone buzzed.

Damn!

She withdrew her hand and reached for the phone. It was a message from Carson to her, Barry, and Marty. The note was short and to the point. She read it to herself, then again in a whisper as the enormity of the message hit home. She could almost hear God laughing at the three of them again, chortling at the brutal irony of their folly.

Carson's text stared up at her.

TANNER HAS AGGRESSIVE PANCREATIC CANCER. LESS THAN 6 MONTHS TO LIVE.

Son of a bitch! I've got to scratch him off both bucket lists at the same time? Fucking cancer. I hate you!

It took a real effort for her to withdraw the syringe full of epinephrine from the IV port.

No heart attack for you and no items scratched of my bucket list. But a handy... They sedated the shit out of you, didn't they? She giggled mischievously and pulled back the sheet.

Chapter Thirty-Eight

Barry

Barry stared at the paper bag lying on the poured concrete back porch of Lena's rental. *Liquid courage in a bag,* he thought. He'd been looking at it for a solid thirty minutes, reaching for it then stopping over and over again, his hand getting closer and closer to it each time.

Just pick it up. Come on, just pick it up.

He finally took hold of it, twisted off the cap, and poured a slug down his throat. He knew nothing about whiskey brands and had planned to buy a pint of anything that appealed to him at the lowest price until the liquor store clerk pushed a bottle of Burton's Premium Whiskey toward him. It burned his mouth and throat on the first swallow and only got worse from there. It smelled like burnt remains. The first sip tasted like a blend of lighter fluid and laxative, or so he imagined, but he needed courage more than he hated the taste so he continued to drink, alone under the stars with the sound of cicadas loud in his ears. The more he drank, the better it seemed to taste. Or rather, the more he drank, the less objectionable it became.

All that changed when he was halfway through

the bottle. The whiskey began to taste like sadness and regret with hints of confusion and melancholy. He drank further and tasted the finish, all-encompassing bitterness and misdirected rage.

The past weeks had been among the best and worst in recent memory. There was his fling with Lena and the stupidity of planning the murder of a dying man—two extremes by his measure, neither of which had brought satisfaction.

And now Lena was gone. The house had been silent the entire time he'd been there, dark and still with no one moving within. He'd peeked into the rickety garage and found the old truck exactly as they'd left it after the failed attempt on Tanner's life.

It seemed as if she was gone for good. He hadn't heard from her and she hadn't been to work. *Back to Arkansas, I guess. But why? What happened?* The memories of them lying together were still fresh enough for him to relish. He could almost feel the touch of her skin and smell the aroma of her perfume. He wondered how long he'd be able to call up those feelings and lamented that they wouldn't last.

He took one long last slug before casting the bottle away. He stood abruptly and went to the door. Then, as he'd witnessed on film, he covered his fist with the sleeve of his jacket and punched out the pane of glass nearest the doorknob. Reaching in, he twisted the latch.

Look at that, he thought with his alcohol-saturated brain. *It works.*

He stepped in. The darkness and emptiness closed in around him. It felt so eerie it was palpable.

Palpable but silent. Closing the door behind him, the crackle of the cicadas died off considerably.

There was no sign of her in the kitchen and living areas. He was quick to notice the flashing LEDs on the answering machine. The readout didn't flash the number of recorded messages but instead the indicator blinked FULL. He played back a few of the messages and heard his own voice again and again as well as that of the diner's owner asking if she was all right and when she was planning to return to work. He auditioned several more, jumping to the next and then the next without waiting to hear the full message. They were all alike, except his messages grew ever more pitiful. The diner owner's became clipped and angry, ending with him firing her. "Your check's here. Come pick it up."

There were no clues as to where she'd gone in any of the messages. He gave up on the answering machine after the final message and walked toward her bedroom. There was a stale tang in the air that grew stronger as he approached the bedroom and stung his nostrils, annoying him almost as much as the howl of the cicadas. *Fucking bugs*, he swore in his drunken rage. *And that smell*. It wasn't until he pushed open the bedroom door that the stench of death hit him squarely in the gut and he realized it wasn't the cicadas he was hearing all along, but the buzzing of thousands of flies and maggots.

Chapter Thirty-Nine

Serena

Serena was parked down the block and across the street when Barry ran from Lena's house with his expression screaming terror.

She'd smiled to herself the entire time he was inside, imagining everything he touched, all the evidence he'd left for the police. Fingerprints? Definitely. DNA? Likely. Fabric traces, shoe imprints? Yes. Yes! Did he kiss her goodbye?

I'm sure he touched her. Held her.

She was happy as a lark as she picked up her scrapbook and gazed at the patchwork cover with the title *Antiquing Trips* stitched into the cover with fluffy red yarn.

Poor Barry—such distress. Maybe he'll kill himself. All the loose ends getting tied up in one pretty little bow after another. *Just like my needlework.* She sat up straight. *I hope he does. Otherwise . . . I can't have him incriminate me, now can I? He's always been the good one. Do the right thing, Barry. Be a dear and save me the trouble, would you? Poor, poor Barry. I wonder what went through his mind when he found her with her throat slit, lying on the bed where they'd made love. Probably left a sample of his dinner spewed right on top of her.*

Dear, dear, dear. Absolutely grisly.

She hoped the police wouldn't pay too much attention to the case. It wasn't like Lena was rich or important. They'd see that jalopy in the garage, the junky place and her black roots and get the picture—some white trash floosy got mixed up with the wrong element. Any commanding officer worth his salt would tell the assigned detectives to do the bare minimum, then close the file and move on.

She opened her scrapbook and began flipping merrily through the pages of photos, each one surrounded with keepsakes secured to the thick paper with glue or stitching. Four years of joyful trips were memorialized between the front and back covers of her beautifully decorated book.

Page One captured a special needs teacher, Martha Lundquist, lifeless on the linoleum of her country kitchen. Her belly had been sliced from sternum to pubis and her intestines pulled out with a crochet hook. Still covered in dried blood the crochet hook had been whip-stitched onto the page.

She grinned again after flipping the page to the next one, which depicted a social worker, Joyce Cole, also dead, with a dreadlocks latch through the temple. The photo was complimented with the latch and a dyed-blonde dreadlock from the victim.

Page Three . . .

Serena eyes popped open. She realized she'd done her job too well. The answering machine had to be filled with dozens of messages from Barry. There was no question the police would interrogate him. From there they'd match his prints and DNA to those found at the murder scene.

He's weak, she thought. *He'll tell them everything. And so will the other two. Sissies all of them, weak-minded men with no backbones. Would Carson or Marty running their mouths be enough for the cops to take my DNA as well?* She didn't think so, but couldn't risk it. *That would be terrible*, she realized. *Eighteen-murders terrible, and every ounce of evidence sitting right here on my lap.*

That's not jail time.

That's death row.

She'd have to keep a close eye on Barry, and this case. If the police showed too much interest, or if Barry wavered…

She flipped through the scrapbook until she reached the last completed page that bore a photo, Lena, a waitress, covered in blood lying in her bed. A swatch of her diner uniform was pasted alongside the photo. She had monogrammed a cupid heart and arrow on it along with the words *Barry loves Lena.*

She wasted no time turning the page and quickly counted the empty pages left in the book.

"One, two three," she said with verve. "That's just right."

Chapter Forty

Marty

"Double bounce!" Carson shouted. "My point."

"That was one bounce," Marty argued.

"No, it hit the floor right next to the wall first, then again right in front of you. That's a point, Stitch. Quit cheating."

Marty gave Carson a long hard look. "In what possible world does geometry and physics work so that this ball bounces on the floor and then continues at that angle?"

"The eyes don't lie. My point. Serve it up."

Marty shook his head. He let his racquet dangle from the wrist strap and headed for the door.

"Whoa!" Carson yelled. "What the hell? Where are you going?"

"I'm done playing with someone who cheats."

"So you're *quitting?*"

"Yeah, for good. Find someone else to cheat and bully. I'm sick of it."

"Hey, hey, hey," Carson cooed at him, trotting over to block his path. He raised his hands, placating. "Easy, Stitch. I'm sorry. It's all in good fun."

"It's not fun. And don't call me Stitch."

"What? You love it."

"I hate it." Marty glared at him defiantly. "I hate that name, and I hate that you gave it to me because I was so poor in college I had to sew patches on my old clothes so they'd last longer."

"Marty..."

Marty wasn't finished. "Most of all, I hate how you treat me. And if there's one thing I learned in this huge fucking mess we've been through, it's that I don't have to take it."

Carson stared back at him, slack-jawed. Finally, he managed, "I . . . I never knew."

"That's because you don't pay attention to anything about anyone unless it benefits you somehow." The words felt good to say, and Marty felt a little weight leave his shoulders as he said them. "You've always been that way, Carson, and maybe you always will be. I don't know. But I know I'm done putting up with it."

"I'm . . . I'm sorry." Carson still looked dumbfounded. Marty wondered how it was possible for him not to know these things about himself. *Then again,* he mused, *does a tiger know he has stripes?*

"You're *not* sorry," he told Carson. "At least not for the right reasons."

Carson shrugged. "What are the right reasons? I mean, things are all messed up, you know? Look at Tanner. I spent all that time hating him. Then we spent all this time and effort trying to do him in, when all we actually had to do was wait another six months and cancer would've done the job for us. And now I don't know whether I still even hate the guy or not. First I hate him, then I feel like an asshole and I don't anymore. But if I wait a little while, I hate him all over again. What's that about, Marty?"

Carson looked lost. Marty didn't understand the change of heart. A little pity for the whole pancreatic cancer thing, maybe. But a complete turnaround? He figured it was because Carson's grievance had never been that powerful to begin with. It was money, and pride, that was all. Nothing meaningful, like love.

If he'd stolen your wife, you'd feel differently.

"Do you mind stepping out of the way?" Marty asked. "I'd like to leave."

Carson shuffled aside slightly, shaking his head. "Geez, Marty, I don't want you to go. I didn't realize . . ." He stopped, then sighed heavily. "Man, I'm sorry. Does everyone think I'm a jerk?"

"You mean, Barry, who you call a retard? Or Serena, who you occasionally sleep with but know nothing about? Or Tanner, for that matter, who bailed out your degenerate gambling ass and got nothing but hatred as a thank you?"

"Yeah, those people," Carson said. "Do they think I'm a jerk, too?"

Marty stared at him, trying to decide if he was serious. He couldn't make up his mind if Carson was being stupid or sarcastic. Both were in his arsenal.

Then Carson said, "I really am sorry. I . . . I'll change. I'll change how I treat you, and the others."

"No, you won't."

"I will. I really will." His voice thickened slightly. "You're my friend, Stitch."

Marty scoffed. "See? I asked you not to call me that. You can't even do that one thing?"

"Oh, shit." Carson waved his hands. "Slip of the tongue, out of habit. I'll work on it."

Marty hesitated. Having a backbone felt good. But when he stopped to think about it, how many friends did he have? Just the three of them, really. Maybe Carson *could* change. After all, Marty himself had changed, though perhaps not enough.

I can't keep hating Tanner, Marty realized. *Or being angry at Carson.*

He had to let it go, and try to be a better person in the bargain. Andrea was beyond him forever now, and somehow that knowledge cemented this new direction for him.

He jerked his wrist and grabbed the racquet when it hopped up toward his hand. "Okay," he said. "But I'm serious about this shit. Things gotta change."

Carson pointed a finger at him, cocked his thumb, and dropped it with click out the side of his mouth. "You got it, Stitch."

Chapter Forty-One

Tanner

He was alone in his bedroom, but only because Andrea thought he was asleep. Anytime he was awake these days, someone was there with him. Usually Andrea, but sometimes one of the nurses they'd hired to attend to him. He'd had visits from clergy, whose efforts he appreciated despite not believing their doctrine. The preliminary meetings with the hospice agent had been more fruitful. Knowing that Andrea wouldn't have to deal with many of the details of his impending rapid decline helped him rest more easily.

The light slanted through the roof window, splashing across the table along the far wall. Since the master suite had walk-in closets, they didn't need dressers, and so Andrea had insisted on a picture table. Family and friends from all four decades of their life were arrayed there. From where he sat, he couldn't make out the individual photographs, but it didn't matter. He knew them all by heart.

Tucked in the corner, slightly obscured by one of him and Andrea kayaking in Colorado, was a small framed shot from his college years—him and the fearsome foursome. Fate, mostly in the form of class schedules, seating arrangements, and dorm assignments, had brought them together. They'd shared dinners and drinks and laughs and dreams. Even defied their families to spend Thanksgiving together their senior year. He remembered it as one of the best holidays ever. For a long while, those people had been the most important ones in his life.

When had that changed? He wondered. More importantly, *why* had it changed?

He supposed it was different for each of them. Barry's injury had been his fault. He'd been short-sighted, struggling to save money wherever he could to keep the company solvent, and ensure the Santo Corp acquisition went through. The resulting tragedy was life changing for his friend. Barry had been such a bright and energetic man before that happened, not only keeping the Chismo IT department running smoothly, but forging a tight-knit crew with his vivacious personality. A very different man emerged from the surgeries that saved his life, or at least, a man with obstacles in the way of letting who he used to be shine through.

Tanner wished he could take back that decision, but he couldn't. So he'd tried to make it up to Barry, sticking with him long after every single member of the IT department had reached their breaking point. It was the least he could do. It took a racism complaint that went all the way to corporate to get him to finally give Barry the ultimatum.

His relationship with Carson going south was a little more baffling. He'd thought he was helping his friend out when he bought out his share of Chismo. Carson's gambling debts had always been a joke amongst their group, but that was when losing a hundred bucks was a catastrophe. The kind of money Carson owed by the time he came to Tanner was ungodly. Even worse, the people he owed weren't going to write off any losses if he couldn't pay. They'd write Carson off instead.

So Tanner paid him a premium for his piece of the company, bailing him out. He had to leverage most of his own personal holdings to do it, and it put the company on precarious ground, but it was worth it to him. That was what friends did for each other.

Carson started to grow distant almost immediately, and after the Santo Corp acquisition, stopped coming around entirely. Tanner supposed it was the man's pride that did it. Carson was hugely competitive. The way things worked out must have seemed like a loss to him.

Tanner wished Carson hadn't seen it that way. He would have offered him a Sales VP position with the company under Santo Corp, but by the time the opportunity was there, it was clear to him that Carson wanted no part of it, or him.

And so he lost another friend.

Marty was the easiest to understand. The two of them started drifting apart after college anyway, though not intentionally. Life's pursuits just had them going in different directions. He'd been glad he could throw business Marty's way every quarter for tax work. It gave them an opportunity to catch up. Maybe not every quarter, but a couple times a year, at least.

Then came the massive party to celebrate the Santo Corp acquisition. Marty had arrived, and for the first time, he brought Andrea along.

Andrea. Tanner took a deep breath and let it out. His heart still ached in a good way every time he thought of her. It had been that way since the first minute their eyes locked, like one of those stupid rom-coms that he never used to watch and always mocked. But then she walked into the room, gave him one look, and he was gone, gone, gone over the rise.

Still, if she'd been happily married, that's where it would have ended. He had no desire to hurt Marty, a guy who had soft enough feelings as it was. But later, he'd stepped out on the balcony to get some fresh air, and she was there, upset about something. They talked, and it all spilled out. She was leaving Marty. It was over.

He didn't regret what followed, except for all the pain it caused Marty. He wished he could have sat down with him, man to man, and told him the truth of it. Would Marty have believed him? Probably not. And when the army of tax lawyers employed by Santo Corp took over the work Marty had done as a contractor, it severed their last connection.

He didn't know how to make it right. Lying there in his bed, staring at the slant of sunlight as it reflected off the glass of the framed photographs on the table, it seemed important to him. To make amends.

Even Serena, who had remained with Chismo as the head of HR, became distant after the acquisition. He assumed it was because of Andrea. Any time there's a divorce, people seem to think they need to choose sides. Serena chose Marty, and her usual cool demeanor toward Tanner became almost frosty.

She'd always been strangely aloof, though. Her enigmatic behavior was compelling, almost sexy, and Tanner had to admit, he'd fantasized about her a few times. But even more than that, he wished now that he'd gotten to know her better. Learned about the real Serena, and been a better friend to her. Maybe he and Andrea could have joined her on an antiquing trip or something.

He closed his eyes for a moment, and was surprised at how difficult it was to open them again. The doctors had warned him about that. Between his recovery from the car striking him and the aggressive progress of the cancer, he was going to be weary almost every moment.

I still have a little time, he thought. *I can still set things right.*

His four lost friends. Maybe, in the time he had left, he could find a way to find them again. Because, in the end, what was more important than true friends?

Epilogue

Nine Weeks Later

Marty

There was no rain for Tanner Fritz's funeral, but no sunshine, either. The day was slightly overcast, hovering on the border of jacket weather. A slight wind blew and it was brisk enough to make Marty feel a little cold in just his suit coat.

He stood in between Carson and Barry as the priest spoke while the groundskeeper lowered the casket into the ground. Some sounds of muted weeping came from the assembled crowd, but many were smiling wistfully. That was because the memorial immediately prior to the burial had been strangely upbeat. Andrea had specified that Tanner wanted it to be termed a 'remembrance party' and that his final wish was for everyone to smile and get drunk on his tab. A professional video commemorating Tanner's life was set to all his favorite songs, and only the one centering on his love for Andrea was sappy. All the rest had beat and rhythm, livening up the many pictures of a beaming Tanner engaged in living the full life that he had.

No Dibs On Murder

Marty stole a glance at Andrea as the casket reached its final resting place. She stood erect in her black dress, neither fighting back tears nor overcome by them. He admired who she had become, and wondered if she'd have turned out to be that same person if they'd stayed married.

Probably not, he decided. He hadn't been good for her in the same way Tanner was. He saw that now. And while the revelation hurt, the blow had been softened by events the previous day.

He'd been surprised when Tanner's estate lawyer asked him to come to his office. Finding Carson and Barry there had been even more surprising. But nothing prepared them for the shock the lawyer hit them with in the meeting that followed.

Tanner had left each of them a minority share in Chismo, and designated them as Vice-Presidents of their own division. Marty had finance, Barry IT, and of course, Carson had marketing. He learned that Serena's HR position was converted to VP status, as well.

He looked around for Serena, but didn't see her anywhere. As yesterday in the lawyer's office, she was absent from the service today. In fact, she'd been strangely distant since they got the news of Tanner's cancer nine weeks ago. Marty didn't worry about it. Everyone processed grief in their own way.

Grief. As the assembled throng started to break up, Marty almost smiled at that. Up until recently, the thought of Tanner's death would have given him a grim satisfaction. But when he learned the man had actually passed away, it was true grief that Marty immediately experienced. The only thing to nudge it momentarily aside at all over the past few days had been his surprise at Tanner leaving them shares in the company and making them all vice presidents.

But it was once again full-fledged grief he felt now. A quick look at Carson and Barry told him they were feeling it, too. It was the strangest thing and it kept them all standing at his graveside. He wondered if there was a rational way to explain it. He didn't know. All he knew was that Tanner Fritz was gone, and he grieved for the man.

Some might say he needed to forgive Tanner so that he could move on. His therapist had urged exactly that. Marty had come to realize, though, that there was nothing to forgive. Not once he removed the blinders of his own hurt feelings and truly looked at the situation. Tanner hadn't wronged him, nor stolen anything, at least not purposefully. Life had simply happened, and Marty's own feelings were collateral damage.

He'd learned something from what he'd been through. Losing Andrea, and all the macabre planning with his friends, had eventually pushed him to a strange place, one he never thought he'd be. And even stranger yet, when he talked to Carson and Barry about it, they both admitted to feeling the same way.

I want to be a better person, he thought. *I need to be a better person.*

It wasn't profound. It wasn't deep. It wasn't even particularly original. But it also wasn't something that had even remotely crossed his mind in a very long time. Now, it was his life goal.

He could thank Tanner for that.

Carson rested his hand on Marty's shoulder and gave him a comforting squeeze. Together with Barry, the three of them walked away from the gravesite toward their cars.

A new and better life awaited them.

Serena

Serena had liked the feel and flavor of Flagstaff, Arizona, with its blue skies and dab-like fluffy clouds. It still smacked of the Wild West. Men and women wore ornate cowboy boots and had no reservations about holstering their sidearms in gunbelts. Indians sold trinkets and handcraft from roadside stands.

The hustle and buzz of work and the drama surrounding the reckless planning to eradicate Tanner Fritz had been pushed from her mind. She was determined to keep it at bay as long as possible. One of the perks of heading up HR was knowing the benefits package inside and out. She was determined to enjoy every moment of her paid grievance leave and maybe quite a bit more. She was a corporate VP now with equity. Who knew how far she could push it?

She'd met Kylie while visiting the Grand Canyon, a woman with little to live for, a woman who couldn't see a future for herself. It was a shame, really. Kylie was pretty and well educated, but like other women Serena had known in college, she'd fallen for the wrong guy, a cheater, who after three years together left her the day she told him she was pregnant. The pregnancy didn't go to term. She lost her "Little Avocado" at sixteen weeks. She told Serena that she'd come to the Grand Canyon to take her life, to plunge into the mile-deep abyss and put an end to her suffering.

Gutless or courageous? Serena wondered. *Afraid to face the future but strong enough to take the big deadly leap. Jury's out on that one.*

Kylie didn't have the guts to see it through but what she lacked in courage Serena more than made up for. They had dinner together that night. The next day, Kylie filled a page in Serena's scrapbook. On her page along with a photo of the deceased woman Serena had embroidered the word MERCY.

She was leaving for the Painted Desert in the morning, determined to take advantage of the dusty hues that blessed the parched land. There were still two empty pages in her scrapbook and she was determined to fill them before returning to work. She'd use the mauve and sienna colors to accent the next two entries and was eager to find suitable candidates.

Those pages had been reserved for Barry, Marty, and Carson, first and foremost because they could implicate her in the failed murder conspiracy. Though they never succeeded in terminating Tanner, the last thing a serial killer needed was the authorities getting chummy, meddling in her business, looking into matters she needed to keep secret. If they ever got her DNA on file, the matches that would come back would crash their police department servers.

All that, however, seemed trivial after Tanner passed away of natural causes. *The boys can keep*, she thought. Like a good scotch she'd give them time to ferment.

The police had questioned Barry in regard to the murder of Lena Southard aka Lena Pretty, but there ended up being no case to be made against him. Despite the fact that his DNA was all over her place, Barry's alibi was solid. Serena didn't know exactly how the interviews with the police went, but she imagined his genuine distraught reaction probably played well. The police seemed to have done exactly as she had predicted they would. After initially going through the motions, they appeared to have lost interest once faced with the dead ends in the case. Barry was crossed off the suspect list, and he hadn't spilled, so that earned him a temporary reprieve.

But only temporary. He was still too big of a risk.

Carson, as she saw it, was a bad-to-the-bone prick, who would never change. He deserved to die.

And Marty was just plain pathetic, another one trick pony that was incapable of growth.

"One, two, three," she muttered.

Time will tell, she thought. *Time will tell.*

She was sitting in her car with the telltale scrapbook on her lap when she spotted two young women. She sensed the quickening of her pulse and felt her heart beat more forcefully. They were browsing a display of dream catchers from a roadside curio stand. One had jet-black hair, the other bleached platinum blonde. Their uniforms were similar – cutoff jeans, torn fishnets, face piercings, the whole grungy enchilada.

That'd be a real test for her, and a first. Two at the same time.

No room for the boys in my book, she lamented. Then, as she ran her hand over the fabric-covered tome, a smile spread across her face.

Who's to say I can't start another?

ACKNOWLEDGMENTS

The authors would like to thank:

Eddie & Stacey Frederick, who knocked around early ideas and whose contributions led to a couple of plots;

Brian Frederick, whose discussions also added a few sprinkles of humor;

Kristi Scalise, for countless conversations that included what was good and what wasn't;

Jill Maser and Colin Conway, for pointing out all the things that were wrong with it when we thought we were done;

All of our early readers, including Frank's Beta Squad, who picked up all the errors, large and small, who did some laughing and some finger-wagging. You know who you are and you are all awesome.

ABOUT THE AUTHORS

Lawrence Kelter is the author of several bestselling mysteries and thrillers. Learn more about him at lawrencekelter.com and my-cousin-vinny.com.

Frank Zafiro was a police officer from 1993 to 2013. He is the author of more than thirty crime novels. In addition to writing, Frank is an avid hockey fan and a tortured guitarist. He lives in Redmond, Oregon. You can keep up with him at http://frankzafiro.com.

Made in the USA
Middletown, DE
11 May 2021

39465579R00161